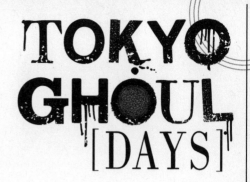

TOKYO GHOUL [DAYS]

SUI ISHIDA
SHIN TOWADA

TOKYO GHOUL-HIBI- © 2013 by Sui Ishida, Shin Towada
All rights reserved.
First published in Japan in 2013 by SHUEISHA Inc., Tokyo.
English translation rights arranged by SHUEISHA Inc.

DESIGN. Fawn Lau

TRANSLATION. Morgan Giles

Library of Congress Cataloging-in Publication Data

Names: Towada, Shin, author. | Ishida, Sui. | Giles, Morgan,
    translator.
Title: Tokyo ghoul : days / original story by Sui Ishida ; written by
    Shin Towada ; translated by Morgan Giles.
Description: San Francisco, CA : VIZ Media, LLC, [2016] |
    Series: Tokyo Ghoul light novels book series
Identifiers: LCCN 2016032597 | ISBN 9781421590578
    (paperback)
Subjects: | BISAC: FICTION / Media Tie-In.
Classification: LCC PL876.O78 T65 2016 | DDC 895.63/6—dc23
LC record available at https://lccn.loc.gov/2016032597

Published by VIZ Media, LLC
P.O. Box 77010
San Francisco, CA 94107

Printed in the U.S.A.

10 9 8 7 6 5 4 3 2 1
First printing, October 2016

VIZ SIGNATURE

www.viz.com

東京喰種 [DAYS]

TOKYO GHOUL

TOKYO GHOUL

SUI ISHIDA

TOKYO GHOUL
[DAYS]

Novel

ORIGINAL STORY BY
sui ishida

WRITTEN BY
SHIN TOWADA

TRANSLATED BY
Morgan Giles

cast of characters

KEN KANEKI

Used to be an ordinary boy who loved literature, but after an incident he received an organ transplant from a Ghoul and became a half-Ghoul. Looking for ways for humans and Ghouls to coexist.

HIDEYOSHI NAGACHIKA

Kaneki's friend. Big on curiosity, with a sharp sense of intuition.

KIYAMA

Section chief, Occult Research Association. Thin as a beanstalk.

SANKOU

Section chief, Occult Research Association. Doesn't say much.

CAIN

Occult researcher. Participates in activities with Kiyama and Sankou.

TOUKA KIRISHIMA

A Ghoul girl with two sides: violent fury and tenderness. She has a younger brother, too . . .

YORIKO KOSAKA

Touka's classmate. Has cooked for Touka for a long time. Has a timid personality.

MAYUHARA

Touka's classmate. Leader of the pack of girls in their class.

SHU TSUKIYAMA

A gourmet Ghoul with some strange obsessions when it comes to eating.

CHIE HORI

Tsukiyama's classmate from high school. Full of energy and very short, Tsukiyama thinks she's like a hamster.

IKUMA MOMOCHI

A Ghoul who moved to Tokyo in hopes of becoming a musician. Lives in the 20th Ward and wants nothing to do with other Ghouls.

HINAMI FUEGUCHI

An orphaned Ghoul who lives with Touka. Like Kaneki, she loves novels by Sen Takatsuki.

KAZUO YOSHIDA

Works at a fitness club. A rather unlucky Ghoul.

TABLE OF CONTENTS

T
O
K
Y
O

東
京

[DAYS]

喰
種

D

H

O

U

L

[THE BIBLE]

*A*ny guy who has a hamburger steak in front of him and doesn't feel hungry probably has something wrong with his sense of taste.

Big Girl, the American restaurant chain. It's a famous steak place, but my favorite is, without a doubt, the deluxe hamburger steak. It's a proud testament to that land where the quantity of food exceeds dietary requirements. And it's definitely not bland either.

The burger sizzled on the hot iron plate, and the scent of its seasoning hit me right in the gut. When I cut into the burger, so much juice came gushing out. And when those juices heated up on the iron plate, they sent a rich aroma straight to my nose.

But the amazing hamburger steaks weren't Big Girl's only selling point. All around me I could see the waitresses taking customers' orders with a smile, bustling around, carrying food.

Looks must've been part of the recruitment criteria. There were so many cute girls working there it was fascinating. And the tight-fitting uniforms made it all the more apparent. Hygienic, yet hot.

". . . Oh."

I leaned forward in my seat to get a better look at the back of the waitress who kept passing my table. The short skirt of her uniform fluttered, and I got a good view of her nice, thick thighs. The way her black over-the-knee socks cut into her thighs was irresistible. What a delicious sight.

That's the kind of girlfriend I want, *I thought, resting my chin in one hand and stuffing my mouth full of hamburger with the other. With each bite, the flavor took my thoughts that much farther away from the girl I watched in a daze.* Yum. *Without thinking I let out a sigh of admiration.*

Could this restaurant be our promised land, our . . . our . . . what do you call it?

"Aaaaah, I can't remember!"

My train of thought came to a stop, and I pressed my hands to my head unconsciously and leaned back. My sudden eccentricity caught the attention of the diners around me, as well as the waitress I had just been eyeing. But that was out of the question for me now. Whenever I'd come here I'd heard that name, and I liked the sound of it. Why couldn't I remember it now?

"A-are you all right, Hide?" the young man sitting across from him called out, sounding worried. And with that, Hideyoshi Nagachika, a.k.a. Hide, returned to Earth from the personal planet he'd been on.

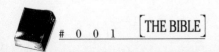 # 0 0 1 [THE BIBLE]

"Kaneki, whaddya call it? That thing?!" Hide said, his index finger flailing violently. His friend, Ken Kaneki, set his chopsticks down. A look of embarrassment and confusion spread over his face.

"Man, it's that thing you're always talking about. This restaurant is our promised land, our Kofi Annan, or Cunaan or something. A Sham Gorilla, where the flowers are always in full bloom."

Kaneki, looking astonished, folded his arms exaggeratedly just like a stage actor and shot Hide a scowl.

"The Promised Land," he said, "is Canaan, and the flowers are always in full bloom in Shangri-La."

"That's it!" Hide said, sticking his index finger right in front of Kaneki's eyes. Reflexively, Kaneki pulled away and unfolded his arms. He kept his look of astonishment as he started in on Hide.

"Like I keep telling you, you should crack open a book sometimes. All right, Hide? Canaan is the land God promised to Abraham and his descendants with his blessing. And Shangri-La is the paradise where immortal hermits live. To mix that up with Kofi Annan or a 'sham gorilla' is just . . ."

"Enough, enough. You're putting me to sleep over here. I've got it now—'Canaan' and 'Shangri-La.' I promise, I'm gonna remember this time."

Looking at Hide as he repeated those words, Kaneki grumbled, "But you'll forget again anyway," and picked his chopsticks back up.

This man, sitting with him at the front of the restaurant, had been a friend of Kaneki's since elementary school. And although they had different majors, they both now went to the same college, Kamii University.

Kaneki was ordinary-looking, of medium height and build. Reading was his hobby, and he was the type of guy who never had friends in his classes. He was the complete opposite of lively, sociable Hide.

"Well, does it really matter that much?"

This consideration was outside his area of expertise. Hide was busy sending looks of love at the waitress with the short hair who had just walked past.

"If I ever get a girlfriend, man, I'm bringing her to this Big Girl."

"Wouldn't it be weird to bring a girl here?" Kaneki said, gulping down some rice as Hide's eyes were drawn to the waitress, deepening his delusions. *The customers here were mostly male. One could say Kaneki's remarks were reasonable.*

"Like hell would I ever want to go to one of those grown-up restaurants or trendy cafes you can't go to without a girl! Taking a girl to a place that I feel a connection to and grabbing a bite to eat would be the chillest thing I could think of."

"You've got a point." On this, Kaneki was in agreement. *And then, as if he had realized something, he grabbed the menu from where it stood on the table, opened it, and showed me a page.*

"What about pasta, Hide?"

"Huh?"

"She could get one of these pastas or something. Like with a salad on the side."

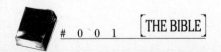

You could say that our inclinations were different. Kaneki's powers of delusion, forged through his reading, were strong. Often he was a far bigger dreamer than me.

"I like it! She'd be eating spaghetti with meat sauce and I could be like, 'Give me some!' And she'd get all mad but she'd be like, 'Well, what else can I do?' and she'd let me split it," Hide said, tapping his finger against the picture of spaghetti on the menu. Kaneki had imagined it even more vividly than he had. "Not bad," Hide murmured a beat later.

"Totally!"

Hide leaned forward and hit Kaneki on the shoulder. Kaneki said, "Ow, man," with a pained smile, then put the menu back where it was before, his eyes creasing with the pleasure of continuing his delusion. *I was also still imagining what this girlfriend I hadn't seen before would look like, wondering what kind of cute girl I'd have by my side.*

"Looks like Ghouls are attacking again."

"Don't the cops do anything these days?"

These unsettling words suddenly invaded the dreamland we were in. We turned our gazes toward the people who were speaking. They were boys not too far from our age, digging into hamburger steaks while talking about Ghouls.

"Ghouls, man . . ." Kaneki muttered, looking absentminded.

Hide poked at his hamburger steak, gone slightly cold on its plate.

"If I met a cute girl who was a Ghoul, I'd still go out with her," he said with a straight face. Kaneki burst out laughing.

"Hide, how desperate are you? Don't give up yet."

"No, man, it's just like . . . how long is it gonna be like this? I need a girlfriend!"

With that their flights of fancy began again. As they ate, they talked about their ideal girlfriend.

Ghoul.

Hide had heard of them, but never seen them in reality—creatures that eat people.

The idea of Ghouls was enough to give anyone a vague sense of unease, but with their random attacks, people felt a sense of distance from them, like they were unpredictable accidents, as though the danger did not actually reach them.

"But isn't spaghetti with meat sauce kind of messy to eat?"

"I think it's all right. Just the once, anyway."

And Rize and I can recommend books to each other!

Kaneki still remembered everything that had happened on that disastrous day very well.

He'd had his head in the clouds, telling Hide all about it. That he'd asked this girl he liked, Rize Kamishiro, to go on a date to a bookstore.

They had met at a café called Anteiku. Kaneki had dragged Hide there before to check her out.

She had glossy black hair that spilled over her shoulders, with glasses that made her look like an intellectual. And yet she had these full lips that gave her a very feminine charm. She was not the kind of girl you'd think was plain but could be pretty if she got dolled up. She was a beauty.

Hide took one look at her and told Kaneki to give up. And Kaneki

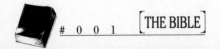

also seemed to see that she was way above his level. But then he wound up getting a date with her.

Hide told him to have a good time and sent him on his way. That was the dividing line.

Instead of the breakdown about the date he was supposed to get, Hide got the news that Kaneki had been in an accident involving some falling steel beams at a construction site and had suffered life-threatening injuries.

With severe damage to his internal organs, Kaneki had needed a transplant—from Rize, who had apparently died instantly.

Miraculously, Kaneki survived. But since that day he'd changed in a few ways.

And this was one of them.

Hide had brought Kaneki to Big Girl to celebrate his recovery when he was finally released from the hospital.

Now, when faced with a hamburger steak, a thing he'd always loved, Kaneki spat it out as if it were foreign substance.

II

When you turned on the TV, the news about Ghouls was incessant.

And people, panicked by this threat they could not see, kept repeating the word "Ghoul," too.

And they were right to panic. In the 20th Ward, where Hide and

Kaneki lived, they'd killed two investigators from the Commission of Counter Ghoul.

The CCG was a special government agency created to maintain security and exterminate Ghouls.

One of those killed had been a veteran Ghoul investigator sent from CCG's head office.

The culprit hadn't been found yet, and the brunt of the anger had been turned on CCG for not producing results.

That said, the streets were still full of people. Objectively speaking, daily life went on. However bad an incident is, people always believe, in some part of their hearts, that tragedy will never visit them.

"Sorry, excuse me. Thank you, sorry." And Hide, cutting through a crowd of that sort of person, was also just pushing through his daily life.

"Man, that smells good." He had arrived at a café with ivy clinging to the façade. Next to the sign on the front, which said "Anteiku," there was a menu.

"Let's do this," he said to himself.

Hide grabbed the doorknob and pushed it open. The scent of coffee, much stronger now, tickled his nose.

The interior, full of green plants, had the calm atmosphere of a place of relaxation.

"Hide!" Kaneki said, his eyes drawn to the door by the sound of the bell when Hide entered. Hide sat down at the counter in front of Kaneki.

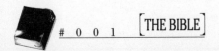 # 0 0 1 [THE BIBLE]

"Hard at work, I see," said Hide, raising a hand in greeting.

"What are you doing here? I wasn't expecting. . ."

"I came for a coffee, man. Hey, by the way, where's Touka?"

"Hard to tell which one is the real reason you're here," Kaneki laughed, as he started making coffee for a customer.

Ever since his organ transplant, Kaneki hasn't looked well, and even now he seems like he might collapse at any moment, but working part time at the café seems to have brought some order to his life.

And similarly, a little while ago, I was in a car with Kaneki and Nishio Nishiki, an upperclassman, when we were hit by a drowsy driver. We were saved by the people at Anteiku. I don't remember much about the accident, but I feel a debt of gratitude toward them for helping me.

He had been especially grateful to Touka, who had apparently nursed him back to health herself. Plus, she was cute.

"Hide, you've got to stop coming here all the time," Kaneki muttered quickly to his friend, who was looking around the café incessantly, searching for Touka.

"Hey, what do you mean by that?"

"Look, it's just, the coffee is a lot more expensive here than whatever you get out of a vending machine, and I'm worried about your wallet."

"That's true, obviously, but you shouldn't even be pretending to drive away a customer! Anyway, one cappuccino!" Hide banged on the counter impatiently. Kaneki sighed as if to show how annoyed he was, and got out a coffee cup.

"That reminds me—I think my British History professor has been getting hair implants."

"Stop, man, you're making me twitch."

Hide's ramblings made Kaneki burst out laughing. With his head resting in his hands, starting to feel relaxed, Hide was just about to launch into a long story when Touka came out from the back of the café.

"Touka!"

Hide's excessive surprise startled Touka, and her smile slipped.

"Why didn't you tell me? If I'd known she was here I would have asked Touka to make my coffee instead."

"Hide, I just finished making this cappuccino. Don't knock it."

Something happened a few days later.

Because Kaneki and Hide's classes didn't line up that day and they couldn't hang out, Hide thought he'd go to Anteiku. *Just to see him if nothing else*, he thought.

As soon as Kaneki, who was taking coffee to a customer, noticed Hide was there, his expression darkened. *I wonder what happened.*

"Hey," Hide said brightly as he approached the counter, pretending for the moment not to notice his friend's mood. Kaneki came over to him, looking around as he did.

"Hide, maybe you should hold off on coming here for a little while."

" 'Hold off'?"

"The manager told us that there've been suspicious characters hanging around here lately," explained Kaneki, looking solemn.

"Did something happen?"

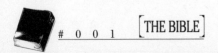

0 0 1 [THE BIBLE]

"Not necessarily . . ."

"Then that's all right," Hide laughed. But Kaneki's face did not change.

He ordered a coffee. As he sat drinking it, Hide's thoughts began to wander. *What is it he can't tell me?*

A couple days later, while sitting in class, Hide remembered what Kaneki had told him. They had been friends for a long time. He knew that what Kaneki had said was for Hide's own benefit. But what did he mean by "suspicious characters"?

"Mr. Nagachika."

"Wha—?"

He suddenly became aware of someone speaking down at him. *The professor saw I was zoning out and came to give me a warning*, he thought, but when he looked up he saw a lanky boy in glasses and a girl with the vibe of a strangely cheerful superhero.

"Oh, where's the professor?" said Hide, blinking uncomprehendingly.

"Class is over," the boy said.

Don't be stupid, Hide thought, but when he looked around the lecture hall few students were left. It was empty.

"Whoa, no way, can I copy your notes?!" Hide grabbed the boy's arm and pleaded. "Please, bro?"

"Sorry, but I'm not in this class," the boy said, tilting his head to the side. Hide asked the girl, too, and received the same response.

"No way . . . If I can't get the notes from anybody then . . . Wait, who are you guys?"

"Finally, you got to the right question!" The boy raised his glasses with a practiced gesture and seemed to puff his chest out as he spoke.

"We're members of the Occult Research Club!"

"Occult Research Club?" It was not a name Hide had heard before.

"ORC, for short. We're an active club, seeking to uncover secrets in this world that cannot be verified using scientific methods. I'm Kiyama, the president. And this is one of our new members, Sankou."

Sankou bowed her head quickly before taking a notebook out of her tote bag. She flipped through the pages, then asked Hide, "Would you, um, not say that your friend Mr. Kaneki is Ghoul-like?"

Hide jolted with surprise.

"Huh?"

"I told you so!"

Next, Kiyama spoke as if taking over the conversation.

"We suspect that Mr. Kaneki may be a Ghoul."

They relocated from the lecture hall to the on-campus outdoor café, where Hide sat facing the other two.

"The majority of ORC is online; we work through social media. Basically, we announce a theme, compile the research topics we get from that in a report, and then present it at a real-life meet-up. So the theme this time was obviously Ghouls."

"So what the hell makes you think Kaneki's a Ghoul? I've been friends with him since grade school, man!"

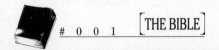

0 0 1　[THE BIBLE]

Without regard for Hide's fed-up expression, Sankou opened her notebook and turned it toward him. It was jam-packed with a list of names, written in small script.

"What is this?"

"It's a list of people under suspicion of being Ghouls."

Hide leaned forward, staring at the notebook. With such a quantity, it was difficult to find Kaneki's name on the list.

"Perhaps you already know this, Mr. Nagachika, but it's said that Ghouls cannot eat human food."

"Mmm, right, Ogura mentioned that in *How to Spot a Ghoul*, didn't he?" Hide said.

Hisashi Ogura was a well-known authority on Ghoul research. If anything to do with Ghouls happened it was as good as certain that he'd be on television talking about it.

"Oh, you're interested in Ghouls, too! That'll make this conversation quicker. Have you seen Mr. Kaneki have a meal lately?"

"A meal?"

"Yeah. This month, we've been investigating whether there is a possibility that some people who have never been seen eating on campus are Ghouls."

"What?! Just because of that?!"

Even recklessness had to have its limits. There must be tons of people who didn't eat on campus.

"We're going person by person collecting evidence at the moment. So, Mr. Nagachika. Have you seen Mr. Kaneki have a meal in the past month?"

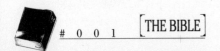

0 0 1 [THE BIBLE]

"We've had a coffee together."

He couldn't understand what was going on, but Hide answered honestly.

"Can't really say he's in the clear, then."

"Wait, hang on now! I mean, we've gotten food together hundreds of times before, just not in the past month!"

"Our investigation is focused solely on the past month. So in that case, we've got others to check out now. See you around."

They did not listen to a word Hide had to say. Now that their task was done, they turned to leave. Their suspicions about Kaneki had not been lifted.

"Wait, wait, wait! Hey, I know!"

Hide slammed his hands against his knees and stood up.

"Let me help your investigation!"

Kiyama and Sankou turned to look at Hide, his fists raised in the air.

III

The members of the ORC were indeed active.

In the same manner as they'd approached Hide, they were conducting a survey of people around campus to confirm whether or not someone was eating.

Their activities were not limited to that. They also checked the patrol routes of the CCG's 20th Ward branch's investigators.

"Because an investigator was killed recently in the 20th Ward, they've stepped up patrols," Kiyama explained as they crept along behind two solemnly patrolling investigators.

"I always thought people who were into the occult just sat in their rooms reading books," Hide said earnestly, trailing behind Kiyama and Sankou.

"We do that kind of research too, of course. But there are some things like this that you've just got to see for yourself."

Sankou, who did not speak much, nodded in agreement. Hide took a glimpse at her notebook. Nearly half the names crammed onto the page had been crossed out. If someone had witnessed the person eating, they were determined not to be a Ghoul and removed from the list.

"Hey, Sankou, come on, take Kaneki off too."

"If Mr. Kaneki is seen eating I'll remove him, but I'd like to maintain the status quo as there's an ORC reporting meeting soon. If we have too few research subjects it's no good."

It doesn't seem like these guys really think the kids on their list are all Ghouls. It sounds bad, but they're concocting these "Ghouls" in order to write a report to submit at the meeting. Too bad for those who get caught up in it, Hide thought.

"Will you be coming to the meeting, Mr. Nagachika?"

"Would that be all right?" Hide asked, tilting his head.

"Everyone's welcome! Come see the culmination of our Ghoul research!" Kiyama enthused.

"Okay, I'll come see it with my own eyes!" Hide said, returning

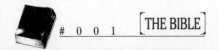

the excitement. But as soon as the other two turned their backs, he sighed.

Sankou's notebook came into Hide's line of sight again. In the end, he couldn't get Kaneki's name removed from the list until the day of the meeting.

Friday, 6:00 p.m. The ORC meet-up and reporting session was being held at a bar and restaurant downtown.

"It's not just students, huh . . ."

The room they had reserved was crowded with men and women of all ages. But although there were many people there, only five groups had managed to put together a presentation on their investigations. And Kiyama's group was the last of the five to present. When their turn came, they distributed handouts to the attendees and began to present the results of their investigation.

Although Kiyama's group's presentation did not get at the heart of what a Ghoul was, they reported that there was an unexpected number of people who did not eat in front of other people, meaning that Ghouls could easily mix with humans without being noticed. This, they concluded, raised the question of how one could uncover the evil lurking within everyday life, putting one's real value as a person into question. Judging by applause, their report was well-received.

After the presentations, the meeting turned into a social event. Suddenly drinks began to flow. If anything, this revelry may have been the main point of the meeting.

"That's it for now!"

The next research theme had been announced, and with that the talk of Ghouls was over. With that load off his shoulders, Hide felt relieved and reached for some bar snacks. His mind turned to more common lines of inquiry, like whether Kiyama and Sankou were dating.

"Hey, guys—thanks. Your research was pretty interesting."

A man in his early twenties, with a beer in his hand, appeared and sat down beside them.

"Hm?"

"Call me Cain. It's what I go by online," the man said in reply to Hide's nonverbal question mark.

"Oh, you're *that* Cain!" Kiyama stood in surprise.

"What? Is he famous?"

"This man is a rising star among occult researchers! There was

that investigation of the mysterious crying sounds coming from the bomb shelter used during the war, and the on-the-ground report from Aokigahara... When it comes to Ghouls, he'll go to the big hospitals and visit the victims' rooms. Any haunted spot, any ruin with a story behind it, he'll go in without any fear to verify the rumors. He's amazing!" Kiyama said passionately. Sankou, sitting next to him, nodded vigorously.

"But let's not talk about me, when you guys are the stars of the evening. Your presentation was very interesting."

Cain turned the group's handout toward himself with a smile.

"I was particularly intrigued by the young man who has eaten with friends before but hasn't been seen eating at all in the past month."

"Eh?"

Hide's eyes widened. The case Cain had taken note of was Kaneki.

"No, no, that guy's totally normal," Hide laughed, waving his hands to dispel the idea.

"How can you say so?" Cain replied.

"Well, man, he's my friend. We've been hanging out since elementary school."

"Oh, so this friend cited as a witness must be you, then. What's your friend called?"

"Ken Kaneki..."

"Hmm. Pretty normal-sounding name," Cain said. "But, you know..." He paused. "It really hasn't crossed your mind? That he could actually be an acquired-type Ghoul?"

The phrase made Hide's heart pound.

"Acquired-type Ghoul? That's a new one on me!" Kiyama said gleefully, jumping into the conversation.

"No, never," said Hide, still pulling himself together. At this, Cain sighed wistfully.

"You've got no sense of romance. Building on the powers of the imagination to make all kinds of hypotheses is one of the best parts of the occult. I mean, I understand—I wouldn't be very happy if a friend of mine were suspected of being a Ghoul. But then wouldn't you do a thorough investigation in order to dispel the suspicion that your friend's a Ghoul? If you were part of the ORC?" Cain's defiant stare was fixed on Hide.

"A thorough investigation?"

"Yes. With everyone thoroughly observing him."

The conversation had turned in an unexpected direction. But perhaps because Kiyama and the others were so thrilled to be working with Cain, Hide unthinkingly said, "Of course!"

What good is it to be a bystander at times like this?

"All right, then! Let's shed some light on those suspicions about Kaneki being a Ghoul!"

The next morning at seven, Hide, Kiyama, Sankou, and Cain met up near Kaneki's house.

"Cain, I'm really sleepy, man . . ."

It was Saturday, what should have been a day off, but they'd all had to get up early anyway. Hide yawned as he grumbled.

"If you don't investigate seriously, you miss out on things. You're

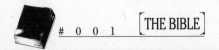

doing this for your friend. You've got to push yourself," Cain said.

"Why are you so passionate about this?"

Hearing Hide's question, Cain folded his arms.

"That's a fair question. Partly because it's interesting, but also, I just love the feeling of getting a few results through trying to solve a mystery. It's not just about the occult, either. I love the sense of achievement I get when I complete a jigsaw puzzle too," he said.

"How interesting!"

Kiyama said he was the same and launched happily into a conversation about the occult with Cain. Perhaps it was lucky to have found an interest they could fall in love with.

"Oh . . . Just a second," Cain said, his voice hushed. Hide wondered what was the matter, and then it became clear that Kaneki had left his house. Sankou quickly opened her notebook.

"I suspect he is heading for his part-time job at Anteiku," said Sankou.

"Wow, Sankou, you've even got details on where he works?!"

"Obviously."

"Mr. Nagachika, do not insult our abilities!" Kiyama said proudly, lifting his glasses.

In that case I wonder if the suspicious characters that have been appearing around Anteiku are actually these guys? It's possible, Hide thought.

"Okay, guys, let's follow him to this café. There's something kind of suspicious about him . . ."

Paying no attention to the conversation, Cain began walking in the lead.

Following Kaneki like this sure feels weird.

If Kaneki spotted Hide he would know immediately that he was being followed, so Hide trailed behind Cain and the others like a shadow, desperately scratching his head.

After that, Cain began his thorough investigation of Kaneki. He worked weekends, of course, and snuck into classes during the week. It made Hide's face twitch to see Cain, seemingly innocent, sitting in the same classes as Kaneki. Kiyama and Sankou, on the other hand, seemed impressed by his passion.

"He really does show no sign of eating. What if we've hit a home run?" Cain reported proudly. He was sitting at the outdoor café on campus, showing no hint that he was actually an outsider.

It would be a huge coup for the ORC if they uncovered a Ghoul. And what's more, plenty of reward money would follow, too.

"No way, man."

Hide was the only one with objections.

"Because you've known him since you were in elementary school? And because you guys have always gone to Big Girl for hamburger steaks since you started college?

"But not remarkably recently, right?"

Cain's face looked composed.

"He was in the hospital not too long ago, and Kaneki still isn't back to his old self," Hide pleaded strongly.

"Okay, okay, calm down, now. I can't be on the lookout twenty-

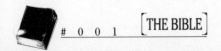

four hours a day either, so there may be something I've overlooked. The late shift of this investigation is especially lacking, and that's when Ghouls are said to be most active."

Just as Cain had said, the majority of Ghoul incidents happened at night.

"Apparently Mr. Kaneki is going to be working late tomorrow, so I think I'll lie in wait for him. Perhaps I'll be able to observe something decisive."

At this, Sankou, who was usually silent, tentatively raised her hand. "I'd like to join you," she said.

"Me too! Of course!" And naturally, Kiyama followed.

"But guys, this could be dangerous. Maybe we should just give it a rest," Cain said, lowering his eyebrows as if he were worried about the two of them.

"We'll be fine," they said, nodding resolutely.

"And what about you, Mr. Nagachika?" Cain asked, sounding troubled, as if he did not want to force him. Hide clinched his fists.

"I'll come along. Because there's no way Kaneki's a Ghoul. Nothing dangerous about it at all," he said.

Hide's words had hit Cain somewhere, because he nodded and said, "Yeah."

"Well, in that case, shall we all meet tomorrow around eight in front of Anteiku?"

Oh no.

Hide's insides felt all torn up.

As the saying goes, he had a bad feeling about it.

And Hide had enough confidence in this intuition to feel sad.

IV

It was the next day, the day they planned to tail Kaneki at night. After his classes were finished, Hide went home for a bit. He kept lying down to rest and then getting right back up again. The chaos in his mind got louder as the time to meet the others approached, and being alone was getting painful.

"Gotta get out of here," he said to himself.

He left the house a little early. The cold wind, somehow smelling of night, slipped next to his skin before rushing back toward the sky.

Looking blankly at the sky, which still showed traces of burnt red toward the west, Hide thought about the old days.

He thought about the school play that had been a success in its own way, that summer night when they'd set off bottle rockets and that old lady from the neighborhood had yelled at them to keep it down, and about the Big Girl hamburger steaks they'd stuffed themselves with to their hearts' content to celebrate getting into college.

Kaneki was part of all of those memories. And it would be the same vice versa.

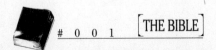 # 0 0 1 [THE BIBLE]

The wind began to blow again. With his arms wrapped around his trembling body, Hide spotted a vending machine.

He stood in front of the machine, staring at the selection of hot drinks. The machine had the type of canned coffee Kaneki preferred. Black, no sugar. Hide knew it was far too bitter for his taste.

He bought it anyway. He clutched it in his hands to warm his cold skin before stuffing it in his coat pocket.

"Huh?"

He'd decided to head where there were lots of people and had just happened to pass by the station. All of a sudden, the sound of someone singing happily stopped Hide in his tracks.

He looked around and saw a street musician singing in the plaza. The song was good but nobody was listening.

Hide checked his watch. Still two hours until they were supposed to meet. He sat down directly in front of the busker. *He's not much older than me*, he thought. The guy noticed him and, giving Hide a carefree smile, he started to sing louder.

"God is there, yeah, don't lose sight . . ." he sang, during the most exciting part of the hook.

"God?" Hide muttered to himself.

"Is something troubling you?"

"What?"

Lost in his own world, Hide was surprised to hear a voice suddenly directed toward him. The musician had stopped playing. *How did he hear me talking to myself?* Hide raised his head in reaction to the musician's question.

"Oh, sorry, man. No . . . I was just thinking what a great song that was."

Hide applauded hurriedly, but he knew that it was pointless to try to keep up appearances with someone who could tell something was going on from one casual remark. All at once, the worries that he'd been keeping locked up inside began to spill out.

"It's just . . . my friend's in trouble and I want to help him but I can't in any big way. Like, it's not going well at all. If there is a God, I need their help."

What's the point in even trying, he thought. *This whole thing with the ORC has become so drawn out because I couldn't stand up to them properly.*

"I see," said the musician, nodding. He was silent for a moment before he spoke again. "But you know, it's okay, isn't it? You don't have to do anything big to help."

"What do you mean?"

"I mean that your friendship isn't based on helping each other, but on being together. To put it simply, you're friends because you enjoy being together."

The musician had a slight accent when he spoke. Hide wondered where he'd moved to Tokyo from.

"Sometimes it helps just to be someone's friend. I think there's nothing better than that," he said.

He hadn't expected to get encouragement from a total stranger. But his words had, oddly, filtered into Hide's mind. Hide nodded as if to say, "You're right."

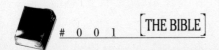 # 0 0 1 [THE BIBLE]

"Looks like you're feeling a little better already! Or maybe I've gotten a little naive!" the musician said.

Hide got to his feet.

"Oh, I should give you something to say thank you," he said, getting out his wallet.

"Keep your money," the musician said. But Hide still felt he had to give him something. He was panicking, wondering what he could give the guy, when he remembered the canned coffee in his coat pocket.

"Sorry, man, this is all I've got," he said.

The can was pretty lukewarm. But the musician's eyes lit up.

"Wow, no way! I know I said keep your money, but I haven't eaten too well these past few days. This helps a lot!" Taking the can, he smiled and said, "God's work."

"Like I said, man, it's all I had," Hide said, smiling back. He bowed his head deeply in thanks before rushing off.

"Uh, where can I get them . . ."

After he left the musician, Hide went into a discount store. In his mind were the memories of setting off fireworks with Kaneki. Hide bought some rockets and a lighter, then headed for a convenience store.

"Hey, Nagachika!"

By some chance, Kiyama was there by the periodicals rack, flipping through a magazine.

"Oh, hey. Killing time?"

"You know me, always gotta be doing something! You?"

"Well, you know."

Hide went on by. First he grabbed a rice ball, then headed to another section.

"Huh? What are you getting that for?" Kiyama asked, his head tilted to one side. Seeing Hide at the register, Kiyama had stopped reading and come over. Hide took the product in his hand as if he were going to crush it.

"Because I wanted it," he said.

By the time they got to the meeting point in front of Anteiku, Cain and Sankou were already there. Cain saw them coming and gave them a small wave, then squinted to try and see inside the café.

"Kaneki's not done working yet. Let's have a look around this area for the time being. We might lose sight of him if we're not familiar with the lay of the land," he said.

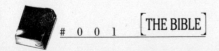

0 0 1 [THE BIBLE]

Most of the streets around Anteiku were deserted. Once night fell they would be all the more eerie, like a haunted house.

Everyone followed behind Cain as he started down the darkening streets.

"Cain? I keep feeling like something's gonna jump out."

Kiyama kept looking around; he was all keyed up and unable to calm himself. Sankou's gaze, too, was restless.

"I know what you mean. I can walk around abandoned buildings or whatever with no problem, but something's got me nervous today," Cain said. *Maybe we shouldn't go too far.*

As Cain spoke, there was a rustling. And the sound was getting louder.

"W-what is it?!"

Trembling with fear, Kiyama turned around—to see Hide taking the crinkly wrapping off his rice ball.

"Oh, sorry. Got hungry."

"Not a care in the world, eh, Nagachika?"

Hide chomped into the rice ball.

"You've got nerves of steel!" Cain laughed.

"You know what they say: you can't go into battle on an empty stomach. But maybe we shouldn't wander too far. A real-life Ghoul might come out at us . . ."

"Hide, are you freaking out too?"

"Yes, I am! Even people who live in this area get lost around here."

"Oh, right. Well, then, maybe we should head back."

Having only just gotten there, Cain started back toward the café. Kiyama and Sankou's relieved faces seemed to say, *Finally*.

But the group had gone down a rather deep alley. And sure enough, they had gotten lost.

"Another dead end, Cain."

Stuck in a narrow blind alley, everyone stopped and looked up at the sky.

"Oh no, lost again . . . Sorry, everyone, just a second while I figure out where we need to go," Cain said, tapping at his smartphone.

It was dark there, far from the streetlamps. There were no lights on any of the buildings surrounding them, nor were there signs of other people nearby.

Kiyama pushed his glasses up, mumbling to himself, "Really does feel like a Ghoul might jump out."

Perhaps his words triggered what happened next.

Suddenly the hairs on Hide's arms were standing on end; he had an oppressive feeling, like he was being suffocated. *What's happening?* But before he'd even had that thought, events were already in motion.

"You're right, this is a great hunting ground!"

The voice echoed in the tiny dead end. Hide looked around to find Kiyama no longer beside him.

He screamed.

Kiyama had not disappeared. He had been thrown back against the wall behind them, slammed against it by the momentum. When

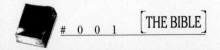

Hide looked back, Kiyama had fallen onto the concrete, as if he'd slid down.

"Kiyama!"

Sankou ran up to Kiyama's body and started shaking him. From the corner of his eye, Hide saw it.

The blood-red eyes.

They weren't dealing with a human being anymore.

"Had to get all the puzzle pieces in place first, but now . . . my dinner is ready!" And there, with a smile of ecstasy on his face and something taillike waving around him, was Cain.

"Hide, I'm one too, I always have been. I'm a Ghoul too! Look, see, it's burned into my eyes! The world you will see at the end!"

With a sound like the wind whipping past, Cain's tail, which had been quivering behind him, grew swiftly. It lightly caressed Hide's cheek before slamming itself into the wall. The wall could not withstand the force: shards flew and dust rained from the hole left behind.

"Pretty scary stuff, huh?! Shake, cry, cower all you want, but look! Look at this!"

His tail, swaying just like a T. rex's, hit the concrete. The sound of the impact went straight through Hide. At the sight, Sankou fell on top of Kiyama as if to protect him.

"Don't worry, I'm not going to kill you yet. I want to enjoy the moment before I take the puzzle apart. What a waste it'd be if I didn't take my time and savor you . . ."

The end of Cain's tail rose up, aiming toward Hide.

"Hey, isn't it funny, Hide?"

Hide turned on his heel and began to run at high speed, leaving Kiyama and Sankou behind.

"I don't think so, Hide. You don't seem like the type to run off and leave your friends!" Cain said, raising his voice as if Hide had disappointed him. He began to head toward Hide.

Hide looked back just for a second. He saw Cain and those gleaming red eyes steadily approaching.

"Dammit, dammit, dammit!"

After turning again to face forward, Hide took full advantage of his knowledge of the area and dashed off, frantically turning left, then right.

"Think you can run from me, Nagachika?"

But Hide's opponent was a Ghoul. Cain stomped the ground and bounded off it, closing the distance between them in one leap. And then one of Cain's tails—his bikaku kagune, a special Ghoul power—struck Hide.

He let out a wordless scream.

The impact was like he'd been beaten with a blunt object. Hide was slammed to the ground. He screamed in pain.

By the time Hide fought through the pain and opened his eyes, Cain was standing over him.

Before his expression had been playful, but now that was gone. His kagune swished through the air as he asked:

"How long did it take you to . . . realize I'm a Ghoul?"

"I didn't, until just now," Hide stammered immediately.

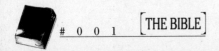 # 0 0 1 ⌈THE BIBLE⌉

"I know that's not true. Most humans freak out and nearly faint as soon as they see a Ghoul. Some start running, but I've never seen a college student like you run straight off. You must have been expecting this," Cain said.

Well, there had been a few things.

For one, when Sankou had noted Kaneki's job at Anteiku, how had Cain known it was a café?

Why had this man, who could handle going into abandoned buildings and places with strange psychic energy, performed absolutely no nighttime observations when that was the most active time for Ghouls?

Once Hide had started thinking about it, there was no end to the clues. And that small sense of unease had built up inside him. But Hide didn't say any of this. Because at this stage in the game, the best-case scenario was that this was a nightmare.

"You're giving me too much credit," Hide said. "All I did was freak out and start running. Just believe me!"

"I'm running late now because of you. All I wanted was to play a little and then kill and eat you, but I'm not from the 20th Ward. If I'm seen invading a local Ghoul's territory it'd be a bad scene," Cain said. He clicked his tongue.

"If I took you back . . . No, you're getting eaten here. It's dinnertime!"

Hide turned his face away from Cain. He hesitated before speaking.

"Please be gentle with me."

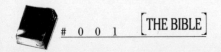

What an idiotic thing to say. I bet he never thought he'd hear someone beg like that, Hide thought. Cain snorted in laughter, and then licked his lips.

"What the hell, man. You were funny, you know that? Been nice knowing you," he said, opening his mouth wider as he slowly approached Hide. Hide stuffed his hands into his coat pockets.

Soon I'll be consumed and then it's all over. Lots of people get eaten like this by Ghouls, I guess.

Cain's breath hung in the air over Hide's face. Then it happened.

Hide pulled his hand out of his jacket pocket and crammed what he'd been secretly gripping into Cain's mouth.

"Wh—?"

As Cain started backing away from this sudden counterattack, he became aware of a foreign substance in his mouth and started vomiting.

"Blech! What have you—!"

Cain was tearing at his mouth with his fingers to remove the substance—the rice ball Hide had bought at the convenience store.

"Ghouls can't eat human food . . . seems like that's all I've heard lately!"

Hide rolled away, putting about five feet between them, before pulling the lighter and bottle rockets out of his bag.

"And look what's next!"

Suddenly he lit one of the rockets.

"Dammit!"

The bottle rockets Hide aimed straight at Cain made a tremendous sound as they flew and exploded around him. Distracted by the bursts all around him, Cain froze for a moment.

Hide seized the opportunity and ran toward him.

He pulled his other hand out of his jacket pocket, and with it, the other item he'd bought at the convenience store. Hide broke the seal on it.

He pushed it into Cain's mouth, squeezing the tube quickly to get all the contents out.

"Hits the spot, doesn't it?"

Hide held one hand over Cain's mouth, and with the other he pushed his chin back. Cain's throat was heaving up and down.

He swallowed.

And then he began to retch. "What the hell is—! It's glued to my throat . . . Can't get it out . . . Can't throw it up!"

Hide showed the empty packaging to Cain, who was thrashing around.

"Meat sauce! Minced meat, tomato, it's all mixed together, like a paste . . ."

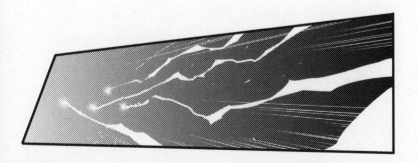

Unlike the rice ball, which was solid, Cain couldn't easily spit out the sauce.

Cain screamed and grasped at his throat. His kagune, which had swollen to show off his power, had disappeared, and only his red eyes remained visible.

"I'll kill you, you asshole . . . I'm gonna kill youuuuu!"

Overcome with anger, Cain glared at Hide, his hands balled up into fists.

But before he could attack Hide, he heard the voice of someone coming down the alley.

"Just what's all this about!"

At the other end of the narrow alley were two men coming their way. Cain's face lost its color at the sight. Each of the men carried an attaché case.

"Looks like this alley's on the investigators' patrol route," said Hide.

Hide, along with Kiyama and Sankou, had followed the 20th Ward's Ghoul investigators. Perhaps it had looked to Cain like they had been running around thoughtlessly, but actually they had been following the patrol route. And in order to draw attention to what was happening, Hide had set off the bottle rockets. It had been a high-stakes bet, but it had paid off.

As soon as the men saw Cain, their faces hardened and they began to shout.

"Red eyes . . . He's got kakugan!"

"Confirmed Ghoul, exterminate!"

Cain began to quake with fear, unlike when he'd been facing off with Hide.

"No, please, don't, don't!"

As he pleaded, something shot through Cain's body, fired from the attaché cases.

"Aaaahhhh!"

A disappointingly quick finale.

Cain's screams in his death throes echoed, but he soon ceased to move.

The Ghoul investigators regarded Cain carefully as they considered when to approach him.

"He's dead."

"Pretty weak for a Ghoul, but who would've thought when we were temporarily dispatched to this area that we'd see a Ghoul right off the bat? Hey, Tojo, give the CCG branch office a call. Oh, right, the kid who got attacked. You okay there, kid?"

The investigators looked around.

But there was nobody else there.

"Spaghetti with meat sauce..."

As soon as the investigators had rushed to the scene, Hide had slipped away.

All he could think about was Kaneki.

When he'd taken Kaneki to Big Girl to celebrate his discharge from the hospital, he'd thrown up when he tried to eat hamburger steak, which had always been his favorite. Just like Cain had thrown up a little while ago.

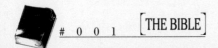 # 0 0 1 [THE BIBLE]

But as if to disrupt his thoughts, he sensed a shadow falling in the darkness. Hide stopped and looked up at the sky.

He let out a wordless sound of surprise.

Fluttering down toward him was a human form.

He had no time to see what the shape was. Shock ran through his mind.

"Thanks."

Hide faintly heard this voice full of gratitude. And that's where his memory cut off.

"Nagachika? Nagachika?"

His consciousness was wrested from the darkness. Someone was speaking, trying to wake him. He tried to open his eyes, but his temples ached piercingly.

"Are you okay, Nagachika?"

He heard the voice again. Somehow he opened his eyes to see who was speaking.

"Oh, good! Do you remember me? I'm Kiyama!"

"Ki . . . yama?"

Still in a hazy state, Hide raised up and shook his head. He tried again to focus on who was talking to him. Behind Kiyama stood Sankou.

"Hey, wait . . . What happened?" Hide asked, not grasping the situation.

"We don't exactly know either."

"Huh?"

"The next thing we knew, we were here."

Not knowing where "here" was, Hide let his eyes wander. He saw that he was sitting on a grassy lawn, not far from a building he recognized.

"We're at the college?"

"Yeah. When we came to we were on campus."

Hide pressed on his forehead, trying to bring back any memories. But he just couldn't.

"And where is Cain? I just don't understand."

Hide jumped involuntarily at hearing that name. Kiyama didn't seem to grasp that something had happened.

Hide glanced at Sankou, but she kept her head down, saying nothing. Was it possible that she didn't want to tell Kiyama that Cain, who he'd admired so much, was actually a Ghoul? Or perhaps she'd lost her memory due to shock?

"I'm not too sure either, man . . ."

Hide rubbed his nose with the back of his hand. He caught a whiff of meat sauce. He sat like that for a little while before eventually returning his hand to the grass and saying:

"Isn't this occult as hell?!"

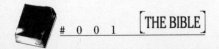

0 0 1　[THE BIBLE]

V

A few days after their mysterious return to campus, the trio compared notes.

Hide said that in his honest opinion it was probably all just a dream, like a crappy movie ending, but Kiyama kept going on about how it was a paranormal phenomenon.

"I guess anything's possible if you live long enough..." Hide said, sounding serious. He and Kaneki were talking after the Asian History class they sat together in.

"What's up with you all of a sudden?" Kaneki said, tilting his head.

"Never mind, man," Hide said, then put his hand to his stomach. *Almost lunchtime.* He was hungry.

He still didn't know what had happened, although he'd managed to convince himself it was a dream or something else. Hide was glad he was the kind of person who could do that. *Maybe I should go to Big Girl for lunch. That place is totally the...*

"Uh, the promised land..."

Definitely starts with a C.

Hide kept repeating, "Ca... Ca..." to himself in hopes of remembering the word. Kaneki just watched, with an expression that all but said, "Forgot it again, huh?"

"Ca... Ca... Ca..."

But the only word that came to mind had nothing to do with Big Girl.

"Cain..."

What he'd tried so hard to explain away as a dream was, after all, all too real. He'd seen a Ghoul—something that had felt so disconnected from his life—up close and personal.

But he was with Kaneki, who would probably just tell him off for being wrong again. And then he'd eagerly start explaining about "the promised land," like always.

"What?"

But Kaneki just sat there next to him, speechless.

"Kaneki? You okay?"

"Hide, have you ever read the Bible?"

"What? Why?"

"Canaan is the Promised Land, and Cain is Abel's brother. They're both in the Bible."

Now it was Hide's turn to be slack-jawed. Kaneki sighed.

"Wait, are you saying Cain's a character in the Bible?"

"It's not a manga, Hide, he's not a character. Cain is Adam and Eve's son. He gets jealous of his brother, Abel, because everybody loves him, so Cain murders Abel. Then he winds up banished to the east of Eden," Kaneki said, then fell silent.

"Hey, Kaneki?"

"Cain used to be seen as evil, you know. Well, I mean, he can be understood as being 'evil' now, too. But if you just think about Cain, you can kind of see that he had to do what he did to be able to carry on, I think. It would've been unbearable for him, you know?"

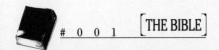

\# 0 0 1 [THE BIBLE]

Kaneki seemed to be telling this story to himself more than anyone.

"But that logic has no meaning before the laws made by God."

The Cain that Hide had known, who was steeped in the occult, must've known that story. And perhaps that's why he'd chosen that name.

But Hide stopped this train of thought before he started brooding. No matter how much he thought about it, he'd still get no answers.

"What the hell, man, quit getting all dark. Here, have some of this!" Hide tried to change the mood, pulling a big bag of snacks out of his backpack.

"Oh, no, I'm good!"

"Dude, just say the word. Look, I'll put them in your bag. So dig in whenever you want," Hide said, not taking in what Kaneki said. He stuffed the food into Kaneki's backpack.

"But it's too full already!"

"Quit worrying, it's fine. Forget about that—you told me about that British History prof before, but man! That baldhead is sprouting new hairs like crazy. You gotta see it! He should be in the library this time of day. It's totally amazing, it's like five poodles' worth of hair at least." Hide stood and started pulling Kaneki up.

"C'mon, give the poor guy a break. Professors are people too, you know." As Kaneki stood there, bewildered, Hide pushed Kaneki's backpack into his arms and ran off behind him.

"Hide, wait!" Kaneki shouted, turning to look, but Hide didn't listen. Kaneki was already out of the classroom when he finally took his hands off his bag.

"Man, you—whoa!"

The backpack hadn't been closed completely, and papers, pens, books, Kaneki's favorite novel, and the food Hide had stuffed in there all spilled out for everyone to see.

"Sorry, my bad!" Hide picked up the backpack, apologizing to Kaneki.

"What'd you do that for?" Kaneki said, putting everything in his bag and making sure to zip it up properly himself this time.

"No, it's just, those guys always go past here at this time of day."

"Huh?"

"Talking to myself. Right, time to go take a look!"

"No, but I said—I don't really care that much!"

After the two of them ran off, two others remained standing in the hallway.

"Guess it turns out Kaneki does eat after all," murmured Kiyama, who'd seen the snacks fall out of Kaneki's bag. Sankou, standing beside him, nodded.

And perhaps that was enough evidence to say that he eats normally.

"Well, I always thought Kaneki wasn't a Ghoul, you know! I mean, how could such a scary creature blend in so well at our college?" Kiyama said, lifting his glasses as he spoke. Again, Sankou nodded.

Then she took out her notebook and crossed off the last name on the list—Kaneki's.

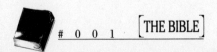

0 0 1 [THE BIBLE]

[**LUNCH BOXES**]

Swaying and trembling on the thin, thin wire of a seemingly endless tightrope.

The first Touka heard from Yoshimura, the manager of Anteiku, that there were suspicious characters in the area was not long after her battle with Mado, the Ghoul investigator.

Touka was taking a break at work when Yoshimura asked her about it.

"What do you think they mean, 'suspicious characters'? Investigators? Do they mean Ghouls? Or humans?" Touka asked.

"I'm not entirely sure. But I do often have the strange feeling I'm being watched, you know. Just something to keep in mind for now, I guess," he said.

She said she didn't know what he was talking about, but

Yoshimura couldn't tell whether Touka really hadn't understood, or if she had understood but was keeping quiet.

If she'd told him that she knew she might not have gotten any more information from Yoshimura, who had ended the conversation and disappeared into the back of the shop.

"Suspicious characters... Maybe I'd better tell Hide not to hang around here for a while."

And Kaneki, who had apparently heard the same thing, seemed worried for his friend who was a regular at Anteiku.

"Why should I care?" Touka retorted. Kaneki looked openly disappointed. *Whatever*, thought Touka. She turned away and pretended not to notice.

"It's just, with all this talk about suspicious people, Hide might get interested in it, which is a scary thought. But if I don't say anything and something happens to him, that can't be undone..." Kaneki rambled on.

God, he's like a girl, Touka thought. But at the same time, she realized just how important Hide was to Kaneki.

Touka felt a spark of humanity within her.

"What if you told him the manager said to make himself scarce for a while?" she said quickly, her back turned to Kaneki.

"Huh?" he said, not having heard her. *Why don't you ever listen?* She cursed him in her mind.

"Stuff like this happens, you know. The manager mentioned suspicious characters hanging around, it's a dangerous situation, blah blah blah, so with that in mind you're warning him to take care.

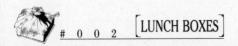

The most troublesome things can happen at times like this," she said. "I should've just kept my mouth shut," she added, then got back to work. Kaneki chewed over her words.

"Back to work!"

"Oh! Sorry!"

You guys are lucky. Things are still good.

She took down orders on her notepad and kept up the faux innocent smile she always wore at work as she tried to go about her usual business, but from time to time a shadow crept over Touka's heart. As she poured a cup of coffee, a memory came to mind.

"Whatever you do to her won't make me happy!"

Her eyes were full of tears, remembering how her friend had looked when she screamed that.

II

It had all started the week before.

"Hey, Touka, tomorrow's a national holiday—we should go somewhere."

Touka Kirishima, sophomore, general track student, Kiyomi High School—that was my position in human society.

I got up every morning just like a person, went to school just like a person, and studied just like a person. Everything I did was perfectly normal. Anyone who said I was a Ghoul would've been laughed at.

Our mere existence was abhorrent to people. And if our identities were discovered we'd lose it all, just like that.

But in the middle of my nerve-racking daily life, where I had to be so, so careful, there was someone whose presence was as encouraging to me as a warm spring breeze: Yoriko Kosaka, who was my friend.

She was sitting across from me at the desk, taking her lunch bag out, when she asked me to hang out.

"Where'd that come from all of a sudden?"

"Well, it just came to me!" Yoriko set her elbows on the desk and put her head in her hands. "What's with you? You're always so busy with your after-school job, so I thought you might like a change once in a while . . ." she said.

Touka lifted her chin, which had been pressed into the palm of her hand. Now that she thought about it, something had been worrying Yoriko lately.

But all it did was make Touka feel like she was being confronted with a reality she didn't want to see. *She started worrying about me after my battle with Mado. You could say that the fight's just being prolonged.*

That sort of bastard just deserved to die.

Every time she tried to rationalize it away like that, the image of the wedding ring nestled on his finger underneath his glove came back to her. *Even he had a family.*

"I mean, am I right? Let's go somewhere!" said Yoriko.

"Yeah."

"Anywhere you want to go? The aquarium, an amusement park?"

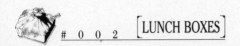 # 0 0 2 [LUNCH BOXES]

Seeing Yoriko's excitement, Touka put her hands to her face. Could Yoriko see it on her face?

"Oh, no, nothing comes to mind . . ."

In response to Touka's vague equivocation, Yoriko said, "Oh," as if she'd realized something. "I guess you go on dates when you have a day off," she said. She'd kept incorrectly thinking that Touka and Kaneki were going out.

"What? I told you, it's not like that!" Touka hit the desk as she rose out of her chair. "Okay, okay, let's go somewhere! We can go somewhere!"

"But . . ."

"It's fine! Just tell me where you want to go!"

Touka ran her hands through her black hair, and her eyes flitted around. Then she hit on the bunny character from the *Zakku-C* series that hung from her phone.

"The zoo."

"Huh?"

"Let's go to the zoo."

The aquarium mainly involved walking around inside, and at attraction parks you had to ride the rides, but at the zoo all you had to do was walk around outside and look at animals. This, she felt, she could deal with much easier.

"The zoo . . . what a great idea!"

"Right?"

"Yeah! And maybe we can see some baby animals too . . . Oh, and they'll have somewhere we can sit outside and eat lunch!"

"Yeah."

"Okay! I'll make the lunches!"

Yoriko was suddenly in action. Touka's face started twitching beyond her control. *This has all gotten completely out of hand.*

I'm gonna have to scout out where the toilets are beforehand, and...

"Let's meet at the station, then! What time's good for you? I wonder what the entrance fee is... Oh—is there any animal you really want to see, Touka? And any lunch requests? Just let me know!"

Yoriko looked happy, miles away from Touka's unease. She was overwhelmed by Yoriko rattling off question after question, and she felt self-conscious.

How can she be so damn cheerful? Touka thought. But at the sight of her friend being so excited, Touka naturally broke into a smile.

Touka reached over and flicked Yoriko's forehead right between the eyes.

"Ow!" she exclaimed, pulling her body up straight again and still smiling happily.

"A trip to the zoo with you." She giggled. "I really can't wait."

"Whoa, they have those too?"

The next morning, when they got to school, Yoriko passed her a map of the zoo that she'd printed from the Internet. "Look!" she said.

Yoriko had come over to share what she'd found out at home: this animal had recently had babies, that animal wasn't on view due to renovation work.

"My dad even printed us some discount coupons."

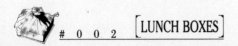 # 0 0 2 [LUNCH BOXES]

The coupons had been printed nicely on thick paper, just like a real ticket.

"Wow, you went all out."

"That's what my mom said too."

So she's been talking to her parents about going to the zoo with me.

"She told me, 'Now don't get too carried away and put Touka in a tough spot.' And that I shouldn't overdo it with the lunches. The menu I came up with was, like, enough to feed five people."

"Five . . . ?" *This is terrifying.*

"Oh, you guys are going to the zoo?" Touka heard a voice behind her ask, pulled in by Yoriko's words. She turned around to see a few boys from their class looking down at the map of the zoo spread out on the desk.

"Oh, yeah, maybe."

"Taking lunch to the zoo, huh. Hey, Yoriko, you can cook?"

Embarrassed by the group of boys, all Yoriko could do was mutter, "Oh, um, yeah," quietly. Touka thought the conversation would end there, but one of the boys continued.

"Yoriko is a good cook. I've eaten her cooking before," he said, jumping in.

"Yeah? How'd that happen?"

"Well, we were in the same class in sixth grade. It was in home ec. She was so good at it, our whole group was totally relying on her. Right?"

"I-it was really no big deal."

She's being humble, but she must be pretty good to have some-one compliment her like that.

I can't share that feeling, and I hate my body for it, but hearing someone say Yoriko's great makes me so happy; it's like it's me he's talking about.

"Totally. Yoriko wants to be a chef," Touka said, speaking for Yoriko, who was getting flustered.

"You already know what you want to do—that's amazing," the boys said. Yoriko was increasingly uncomfortable at so much praise.

When the boys had gone away, Yoriko put her hand to her chest and said, "I was so nervous just then!"

"What did you have to be nervous about?"

"Talking to that many of them at once! But whoever you talk to you always sound like yourself, Touka. I wish I could be like that."

"But you shouldn't be nervous about talking to our classmates, you know?"

"I know. You can just say what you want to say to anyone—classmates, teachers, or even strangers. It must be nice . . ." Yoriko said, looking downcast.

Yeah, I can speak my mind, but does it really need to worry her so much? Touka puzzled it over. Then she pointed to the map of the zoo spread out on the table.

"Anyway, Yoriko, what do you want to see while we're there?" she said, forcibly changing the subject.

Yoriko seemed to be regrouping herself as she looked down at the map, tracing the illustrations of animals with her fingertips.

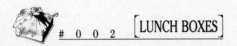 # 0 0 2 [LUNCH BOXES]

Touka hadn't noticed them until then—the eyes glaring at the two of them, trying to keep them restrained.

It happened at lunchtime that day.

We were eating at the same desk as usual, when the group of boys who'd talked to us in the morning appeared again.

"Hey, look at that—Yoriko, did you make that?"

Again, Yoriko was too embarrassed to speak, so Touka said, "Yeah, and?"

"So amazing. Give me some—just a piece," he begged, his hands clasped together. For some reason, Yoriko looked to Touka.

"All right, I mean, I don't care," Touka said without thinking deeply. As if whatever Touka said went, Yoriko passed a little piece of fried chicken to the boy. He stuffed it in his mouth, eating it in one bite.

"Whoa, that was so good!" His eyes were gleaming.

That's one face I'll never be able to make.

"Hey, is it really that good?" Another boy came over, lured in by what the boy who'd eaten the chicken had said.

"Knock it off, Yoriko won't have anything left to eat."

As the boys scattered, Touka thought, *Making someone that happy with her cooking must make Yoriko happy, too.*

But Yoriko's face was stony, and her eyes were downcast.

"Yoriko? What's wrong?"

"Oh, no. It's nothing..."

"They say you're a great cook, how nice!" A girl's voice cut in. Touka turned to look and saw three girls from their class. Although her words sounded in praise of Yoriko, the way she'd said them as if she were insinuating something made Touka furrow her brow. The girls said nothing more but quickly averted their eyes and began whispering among themselves.

"What was *that*?"

"That group of boys is popular with the girls, so that might be it."

Now that she said it, they were all good-looking guys, and what's more, every single one of them was active in clubs and sports.

"But c'mon, that can't be it. I mean, we had nothing to do with them coming over," Touka said with a confidence drawn from thinking everything was fine.

But Yoriko could only murmur weakly, "Maybe you're right."

After lunch, Touka went on her own to the bathroom, vomited up everything in her stomach, and gulped down some water.

When she returned to the classroom, nearly empty since most students had left during lunch, the girls that had been glaring at them earlier were gathered around Yoriko. Just as she wondered what they were talking about, she heard their voices loud and clear.

"You looked so happy when they were telling you how great you were. Is that why you cook, to get boys to like you?"

"Even *you* oughta know that Mayuhara likes Yamamoto. So what are you trying to say?"

"That was so affected, though!" The girl laughed.

"But, I didn't—I never meant to—"

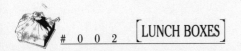

0 0 2   [LUNCH BOXES]

Mayuhara was the girl who had been staring at Yoriko and Touka the most. And Yamamoto was the boy who had eaten a piece of Yoriko's fried chicken earlier.

"What do you think you're doing?"

Touka rushed over to them and started interrogating Mayuhara, the leader, in a firm tone of voice. The other girls flinched at Touka's sudden arrival, but Mayuhara did not move. Instead, she looked at Touka and laughed.

"Oh, Kirishima, you came back."

"I asked you, what do you think you're doing?"

"What do you mean, what? We're just talking. What about it?"

Her faux innocent act made Touka's expression even sterner.

"I heard everything you guys said to Yoriko," she said.

"If you heard everything then you didn't need to keep asking what we were doing, now did you?" Mayuhara replied, only adding to Touka's anger.

"Huh?"

"God, she's scary. Hey, Yoriko, your little friend's boiling over, can't you do something?"

"Oh, uh . . . Touka, I'm fine, so don't . . ."

"How the hell is this fine?"

Touka's rebuke made Yoriko jolt in surprise. Touka slapped her hand over her mouth without thinking, and Mayuhara smirked, looking at her like she was sizing her up.

"Kirishima, you just got mad at Kosaka, didn't you?"

"What?!"

I got frustrated, but you're the one to blame, Touka thought. However, Mayuhara kept on.

"You guys are so different. I bet you get frustrated with her a lot when you're together, don't you?"

"Just shut up . . ."

"And I mean, when you eat Kosaka's cooking you just always look so grossed out."

"What?"

Touka was thrown for a moment by this attack from an unexpected angle. *That's because I can't eat human food. But I can't tell you that.*

"Kirishima, you're the kind of girl who doesn't need anyone but yourself, and there are lots of boys who'd go out with Kosaka. But I heard you two are going to the zoo together? So childish. You can't really be into that."

Touka looked at Yoriko. She had gone pale. Without a second thought, Touka grabbed Mayuhara by the collar. The other girls who were nearby screamed.

"If you say one more word . . ."

"But I don't hear you denying it. I hit the nail on the head, didn't I?"

Mayuhara's words hit Touka right where she was most sensitive— her identity. She couldn't say Mayuhara hadn't the nail on the head.

"How nice of her to stick up for you, Kosaka," Mayuhara said to Yoriko, who was only able to stand there, pale-faced, and look on. Yoriko's eyes were brimming with tears. Touka once again tightened her grasp on Mayuhara's uniform collar, her fists pressed against the girl's chest.

"Seriously, if you say one more word—" *I'll kill you.*

The words were on the tip of her tongue. But before she could say them out loud, she heard a man's voice in the classroom.

"What are you girls doing?"

It was their history teacher, Mr. Tsuruda. One of Mayuhara's friends had gone to get him.

"Ouch! Stop, please, I'm sorry, forgive me!"

The first to react was Mayuhara. She threw herself to the floor, coughing violently, her hands clasped to her chest.

"Wha—"

"Kirishima! What did you do to her?"

Naturally, Mr. Tsuruda put the blame on Touka.

"No, sir, it wasn't like that, Touka was just . . ."

"Ow . . ." Mayuhara whined. "Mr. Tsuruda, sir . . ."

Yoriko again started to leap to Touka's defense, when Mayuhara started wailing.

"Nothing makes me cry! Kirishima, you're just awful!"

"Mayuhara, are you all right? Are you in pain?" Mayuhara's friends got her to stand up as if they were supporting her weight, providing cover for her. All the girls were sharp-tongued. The way they talked, whatever Touka tried to say would come back at her ten or twenty times worse.

"No, it's not—Touka was just . . ."

"Kirishima, staff room—now!"

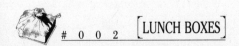

Mr. Tsuruda grabbed Touka's arm and began pulling her after him.

When they walked past Mayuhara, she said, just loud enough for only Touka to hear, "Hilarious."

There was only malice in her words.

"Touka!"

When Mr. Tsuruda's sermon was over and Touka stepped out of the staff room, Yoriko was pacing confusedly along the wall in the hallway. *Did she follow us?*

"I'm so sorry, this is all my fault . . ."

"You did nothing wrong, Yoriko," Touka said bluntly. She started heading toward the classroom, but Yoriko stayed glued to the spot.

"Yoriko?"

Her face was downcast; she had her shirt tightly clenched in her fists.

"Seriously. You did nothing wrong. Mayuhara's the problem," Touka added. "Anyway, I only made her cry once."

I hate when people are always fake like that. And she's the kind of girl that if you turned your back, the same thing would happen again. Before lunchtime's over, I'm gonna settle this once and for all.

"No, Touka, you can't!" Yoriko saw what Touka was up to. "Whatever you've got in mind, you can't."

"Why not? If someone said that to you, you'd hate it too."

"I did hate it. But maybe it's kind of true."

"What? What did you just say? Why would you say that?" Touka heard what Yoriko said as a defense of Mayuhara, and it made her angrier. "Anyway, she's gonna pay for this."

Talking won't get me anywhere.

"You can't!" Once again, Yoriko put a halt to Touka's impatience.

Touka paused. "Yoriko, that dumb bitch wouldn't know something to cry over if it hit her. If we don't settle this she'll think she's won!"

I'm only doing this for Yoriko, so why does she want me to stop?

Her tone of voice, which had ended up sounding like she was yelling, had made Yoriko start shaking.

"I'm . . ."

Yoriko's lips were tightly drawn, as if she were holding back something. But a thin film had formed over her blinking eyes, and the corners of her eyes gleamed in a way that wasn't normal.

By the time Touka realized what she'd done it was too late. Her emotions, running wild in this unexpected situation, started to come back under control at the same speed as Yoriko's teardrops fell.

"I'm happy you care so much, Touka," she said, stringing the words together between sobs without even wiping away her tears. "But . . . but . . ."

The tears spilled down her cheeks in heavy drops.

"But whatever you do to her won't make me happy!"

In my cursed life, the number of people I've crushed is uncountable. All the screaming, the rage, the sorrow. I've experienced extreme situations with all five senses and come through the other side, but here I am, frozen by the words of a mere human, a powerless girl.

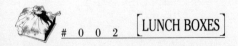 # 0 0 2 [LUNCH BOXES]

There was one more thing.

Why?

Yoriko's tears and cries overlapped, in Touka's mind, with the way she'd seen Hinami cry during the battle with Mado. And Hinami had sobbed, "Revenge doesn't matter to me, I'm just sad."

After that, Yoriko's attitude changed. It wasn't that she blatantly avoided Touka. It was just that she didn't have the same smile as before when they spoke. Touka saw signs that she was trying to say something in her own way, but the words didn't come out.

And it was the same with Touka. She was puzzled by the way Yoriko was distancing herself from her, when she'd always been so gentle and positive toward Touka before.

"Having a pastry again today?" Yoriko asked one lunch hour, seeing Touka opening the plastic wrapper of a pastry from a convenience store.

"Oh. Yeah . . ."

Yoriko's expression was somehow hardened.

The conversation ended, and quietly Yoriko started eating her own lunch. *Before she would've told me I needed to eat more and given me some of her own lunch . . .*

A Ghoul's body won't accept human food, so on a physical level, this was all probably for the best. But on a mental level, it was a completely different story.

And there was Mayuhara laughing with her friends as if nothing had happened. She hadn't really cared that Touka and Yoriko were too close to the boy she liked. When Touka saw her laughing away despite the pain she'd inflicted on them, she was filled with the urge to kill.

Dammit.

It took a day, maybe two, before she saw the solution.

III

"Touka, you're spilling the coffee. Hello?"

Kaneki saw the coffee overflowing from the cup and interrupted her. *Must've been lost in thought.*

"Whoa . . . You should've told me sooner!"

"Uh, okay . . . ?"

Looking frantically for a towel, Touka instructed Kaneki, "You pour the coffee!"

Maybe in time things will improve. If it were me I'd make a very patient decision after a week or so, but the amount of time that's passed now has really surpassed my expectations.

The awkwardness between us just keeps building, like a pebble tumbling down a wintry slope, growing and growing as it picks up snow.

Kaneki made the coffee instead of Touka, and took it to the customer.

"Huh, I don't think I've seen you working here before. Are you new? What's your name?"

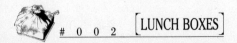 # 0 0 2 [LUNCH BOXES]

"Oh . . . I'm Ken Kaneki."

The customer who'd ordered the coffee looked at Kaneki curiously, then said, "You have a very particular smell about you." Realizing the man had sensed he was a Ghoul, Kaneki returned behind the counter.

"That guy's one of us too?" he asked Touka.

"Yeah . . . He doesn't live in the 20th Ward, though. He's too weak to have a feeding ground in his own ward, so sometimes he comes here to forage. He likes to pry, so it's better not to say too much," she said.

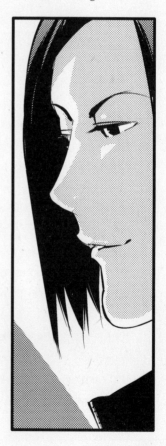

"Oh, right . . . I didn't know there were so many types of Ghouls."

Kaneki looked at the other Ghoul with apparent interest. But his attention soon turned back to Touka.

"I forgot to say, thanks for the advice, Touka. I told Hide not to come to the café for a little while."

"Hmm? What do you mean, advice? I didn't do anything."

"Well, no, but you did give me an example from the past."

Even when I'm cold to him he

still smiles back at me. I think he's gotten a little more resilient. And when Touka's face changed to an irritated scowl, Kaneki sensed he was on the verge of danger and said, "Well, anyway, thanks," ending the conversation.

"If you ask me, he shouldn't come back for the rest of his life," she said in an outburst at Kaneki, who had turned away.

"What?"

"I told you before: Ghouls come here looking for information. Like him," she said, nodding her head toward the Ghoul that Kaneki had just brought a coffee. "He takes humans to abandoned buildings or places where nobody else is, and he kills and eats them. Apparently he's been looking for prey on the Internet lately. But that's the kind of guy that hangs around here. If you care about your friend you should keep him away from Ghouls."

Kaneki held his breath, and his eyes slowly drifted downward. *My words had more effect than I imagined.* Just as Touka started to suspect what he was so at a loss over, Kaneki began to speak in bursts.

"But we've always hung out... This might sound like an exaggeration, but he's like a part of me. If I lost that, I don't know what I'd do with myself."

"Huh? What are you talking about?"

"Didn't you just tell me I shouldn't hang out with Hide anymore?"

Touka had only meant to tell him to make Hide not come to Anteiku anymore, but Kaneki had misunderstood. The logic took Touka aback. If, to keep them from harm, a human friend needed to

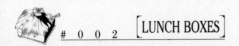

0 0 2 [LUNCH BOXES]

be kept away from Ghouls, then the one they needed distance from, first and foremost, was none other than yourself.

Kaneki's misunderstanding had actually hit at the heart of the matter. *So what about me and Yoriko?*

"Touka, are you all right?" Kaneki asked, clearly having sensed she was not.

"I'm fine."

"You haven't really been yourself the last few days, though."

"It's nothing, I told you."

Now I've gone and made Kaneki worried about me. She felt uncomfortable with his concerned look.

"Is it something to do with Yoriko?"

He'd cut straight to the heart of it. Reflexively she had started shaking. And from that, Kaneki had taken a guess.

"Did you guys have a fight?"

"Just shut up and get back to work."

Touka started washing out the soaked hand towels. But Kaneki did not go away.

"What's with you?" Kaneki asked, sounding annoyed. He looked at Touka as if there were something else he wanted to say. "I hope you guys make up soon." He paused again. "The longer you let things go on for, the more misunderstandings pile up and things get worse. You shouldn't just leave things as they are, in my opinion."

Kaneki had his hands clasped together, timidly offering her his advice.

"You never shut up," Touka fired back. "It wasn't a fight."

On her way home after finishing her shift at Anteiku, Touka took out the map of the zoo that Yoriko had given her and looked at it.

It was only a few days until they'd been meant to go to the zoo. *Things'll be back to normal by then, I know it. And if they're not, if we just go to the zoo anyway, Yoriko will be so happy everything will be just like always.*

Feeling more positive now, Touka carefully folded the map and put it back in her bag.

But betrayal comes quickest when hope is high.

IV

"Huh?"

"Like I just said—let's just forget about the zoo for a while, okay?"

On their break, Touka had spoken to Yoriko, thinking that her friend would talk to her like usual, but instead Yoriko wiped the slate clean, plans and all.

"You changed your mind all of a sudden?"

"Look, I realized eventually that I shouldn't have asked you without taking your schedule into account," she said. Yoriko paused. "So next time—next time we'll go whenever you can take the time. Okay?"

She'd said "next time." But Touka sensed that the truth was there wouldn't be a next time if things went on like this.

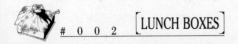 # 0 0 2 [LUNCH BOXES]

"No, there's no need to cancel—can't we just stick to what we planned?"

"Nope. I can see it now, I was way out of line."

Touka fell silent, realizing that whatever she said made no difference.

"See, she won't even say she wants to go," said Mayuhara mockingly. She had been observing them. Touka turned to look at her. "Oooh, scary," Mayuhara said, in an affected manner. Her friends giggled.

"Trying to say something to Yoriko again?" Touka growled.

"Of course not. Just saying what I thought . . ."

Touka made a move toward her, but Yoriko stopped her.

"Next time—we'll go next time. Right?"

Yoriko's weak smile made Touka's heart hurt. *She always used to smile at me so warmly.*

"Yoriko . . ."

It can't go on like this, Touka thought. But she couldn't get the words to come out right.

"Class is about to start! Get to your seats!"

The teacher appeared before Touka could say anything, and then class started.

After school that day, Yoriko left before Touka, saying she had an errand to run. Touka went and stood in front of Mayuhara and her friends, who were gathered around the window of the classroom.

"Oh, Kirishima, not going home with your little friend today?"

Mayuhara asked in mock concern once she noticed Touka was there. The girls were watching Yamamoto's team play out on the field.

"What did you say to Yoriko?"

"What? What are you talking about?" Mayuhara twirled her hair with her finger, playing dumb.

"I asked you, what did you say to Yoriko?" Touka asked in a low tone tinged with murder. Perhaps instinctively sensing how bad this could be, Mayuhara let her hair slip from her fingers. Her eyes flitted around among her friends.

"Nothing. All I said was that it really didn't seem like you wanted to go to the zoo," she said, then paused. "Kirishima, you didn't really want to go, did you? Because if you'd actually wanted to go, and I said that, then you could've easily told Kosaka, 'I do want to go.'"

The other girls murmured words of agreement and support for Mayuhara.

"The same with the lunches Kosaka makes, and all sorts of other stuff. Anyone can see you don't really want to be her friend! If you don't want an outsider calling you out on it, then maybe you should change your attitude? And don't take it out on m—"

A loud bang rang out. Mayuhara was speechless; her friends were left breathless. Touka's fist had gone just past Mayuhara's cheek and connected with the window frame.

What the hell do you know?! Touka was screaming inside. *It's all because I can't eat, because I could be a target at any time, all because I'm a Ghoul!*

No matter how much I try, there's a wall I can never jump over,

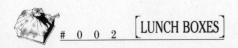

and there's happiness that I can never have. But I'm still hanging on to life. Despite it all.

Mayuhara slid down to the ground on the spot where she'd stood.

"Want to be next?" Touka said, glaring at her and each of her friends in turn.

"I have nothing else to say, so don't, bitch."

Leaving Mayuhara crumpled on the floor, Touka left the classroom.

"Didn't even get to see the baby animals . . ."

Touka walked alone, looking at the map of the zoo that Yoriko had given her.

*Would it have made a difference if I'd said, "But I want to go,"
when Yoriko told me she was calling it off?*

"Hey, Touka. How was school?"

When she got to Anteiku, Kaneki said hello to her happily, not taking note of her mood.

Irritated, she told him to shut up. Kaneki tilted his head and asked, "What's up?"

Touka said nothing.

Kaneki watched her for a little while before asking, quietly, "Did something happen with you and Yoriko?"

She was shaking with anger. She balled her hands into fists.

"And what the hell is it to you?" she shouted.

The customers all turned to look at the same time, and silence fell on the café.

"What is going on here, Touka?" This time it was Yoshimura, who was at the counter, who asked.

"Uh . . . I'm so sorry . . ."

Knowing she was really in for it, Touka apologized. Yoshimura glanced around the café, then said, "Take a little break."

"Wh—I'm fine!"

"Take a look in the mirror."

Touka was dogged in her refusal, but Yoshimura shook his head from side to side. It was a quiet action, but it had a profound power.

Sandwiched between them, Kaneki looked at them both and said, "I think perhaps you should take a little break too."

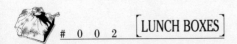 # 0 0 2 [LUNCH BOXES]

Touka was about to raise her voice again to say, "I don't need you to tell me that," but she felt Yoshimura's eyes on her.

"Dammit."

Touka defiantly turned her back and went into the back room.

"God, my face looks awful," Touka muttered without thinking as she looked into the mirror in the living room on the second floor. She had a worn-out expression, as if all the exhaustion in her heart were showing on her face.

"I brought you a coffee, Touka."

Despite her outburst at him, Kaneki had appeared carrying a tray with coffee, acting the way he always did.

"I made it myself," he said, setting the cups on the table then sitting down on the sofa.

"Get back to work."

"Yoshimura told me to take a few minutes."

Kaneki gazed at the coffee, steam rising from it, as he asked, calmly, "Think you guys will make up?"

Touka said nothing. Kaneki chose his words carefully.

"Hey, the thing is, you've obviously got a lot more experience than me in the Ghoul world, and you've taught me a lot, but when it comes to the human world . . . I'm the one with more experience than you."

Silence.

"So, I might be helpless as a Ghoul, but maybe I could be of some use to you in this situation. Just an idea I had."

Kaneki just didn't know when to quit at moments like this.

"How the hell could you be any use?"

"M-maybe you're right. But maybe talking about it would make you feel better, anyway?"

No matter how much she pushed him away he wouldn't leave. Touka was the one who'd run out of patience.

"Go to hell."

She'd lashed out at him again and again, and yet Kaneki still approached her. And she spat words of abuse at him.

She paused.

"If you laugh, I'll kill you."

Touka started to tell him a rough version of the past few days' events.

"Oh, right... that's a tough situation you're in," Kaneki said softly, with a very serious look on his face.

"You really think so?"

"I do! You know how Yoriko is—she must be pretty upset right now." He paused. "And it's not exactly right to call this a fight, but when you have had a serious misunderstanding like this, you can't help but think the worst."

So is that why he said we should hurry and make up?

"But tell me, Touka—how are things, I mean really?"

"How is what?"

"Her sharing her lunch, or the thing with the zoo. What I mean is, what do you think about it?"

I can't keep a poker face when I have to eat human food, and with the zoo, part of it is like Mayuhara said—Yoriko asked me, so I agreed.

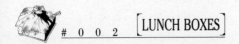

0 0 2 [LUNCH BOXES]

But . . .

"I dunno."

"Right," Kaneki murmured, faced with Touka's inability to provide an answer. "This is something I've felt myself, so some of it might be a little off the mark. But the thing about you is, you always act decisively. For you to feel so lost over something as small as this shows just how big Yoriko's presence is in your life."

Touka said nothing.

An objective, outside opinion. But one at total odds with Mayuhara's.

"So obviously I think you should make up with her. Also, you should go to the zoo. I think if you don't, you'll regret it later."

Originally, the two of them were supposed to go to the zoo the day after tomorrow. But Yoriko had told Touka the plan was off.

"Uh, well, you might be right . . ."

Kaneki cared about Touka and was seriously worried about her. *What a gullible-ass idiot.* Touka traced the rim of the cup of luke-warm coffee with her fingertip.

When they'd first met, he had been screaming and criticizing Touka for being a Ghoul, but before long, when faced with his own tragedies, he'd started to take them to Touka.

"Oh, yeah! Is there anything you could do for Yoriko that would make her happy?"

"Make *her* happy?"

Kaneki clasped his hands, delighted at what a good idea it was, and made his suggestion.

"Yeah. Yoriko's been hearing all sorts of things from people over this, and she's probably losing confidence. Which is why if you tell her how you feel, as if none of that matters, it'll all be resolved."

Thanks for laying it out for me. This stuff is so not my strong point.

"But what should I do?"

"Hm . . . you could give her some kind of present, or write her a letter telling her how you really feel."

"No way. I'm not that kind of girl."

"Oh. I thought that was a good plan."

Kaneki seemed disappointed, and he looked up at the ceiling. Touka brought the coffee to her lips, turning it all over in her mind.

Something that would make Yoriko happy.

What on Earth could that be?

IV

Tomorrow's a holiday—the day I was originally going to go to the zoo with Yoriko.

Looks like my threat got through to Mayuhara and her friends because they're keeping quiet, but Yoriko's still not herself, Touka thought at lunchtime as she ate a terrible sandwich.

When she was given people food it was painful for her to digest

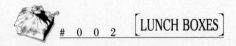

it, but she had loved how sweet it was of Yoriko to give her part of her lunch out of concern for how little Touka ate.

Then there was the zoo. Perhaps Touka didn't really care about going to the zoo itself. But going with Yoriko, seeing her look happy— that would've been enough for Touka. And so they'd settled on going to the zoo, and Touka had loved seeing Yoriko so excited.

"Oh, right."

I did actually want to go to the zoo with her. Maybe it was a different kind of wanting to go from what Yoriko desired, but still, I wanted to go. That's why I've been hanging on to the map she gave me, carrying it with me everywhere.

I should've said I wanted to go when she told me the plan was off.

I'm bad at sorting out my feelings, and although I try to put on a good front I'm just so incredibly immature. And I hate that about myself.

Well, it's not a conspiracy, dammit. If you want to do something, do it yourself, bitch.

The image of her brother, Ayato, who'd left home, flashed in Touka's mind. *I should've said something then, too.*

School ended, and the two of them left school at the same time. Yoriko was talking about something inoffensive, as if trying to avoid anything to do with the zoo.

"Right, well, this is where I turn . . ."

They stood at a crossroads. This was where Yoriko said goodbye. She had always turned off here with a cheery "See ya," but today neither of them was moving very fast. Yoriko seemed to be waiting for Touka to say something. *If I'm going to fix this, now's my last chance.*

But the words just wouldn't come.

"Well then, bye, Touka," Yoriko said, then dashed off, as if she were running away from the silence.

"Yoriko!"

When the words finally came out, Yoriko was already far away, and Touka's voice didn't reach her.

Gripping the strap of her bag, Touka started walking toward Anteiku.

If I use my kagune I can soar so easily, like a bird, like a butterfly. But my feet couldn't be any heavier right now.

"Why am I so . . ."

Thoughts of Yoriko, Hinami, and Ayato ran through her mind, and Touka found it hard to breathe. *All I do is upset people.*

"Oh, and they'll have somewhere we can sit outside and eat lunch!"

She remembered Yoriko's smile. Touka stopped walking and looked back at the road she had disappeared down.

People suck. They're bound by stupid laws, have an idiotic love for groups, and, convinced that they're in the right, they lump together those they hurt and drive them out.

But though they're weak, some of them care about others; they may be fragile, but they show love to the people who are important to them; they may not have claws or fangs, but they will fight to defend someone.

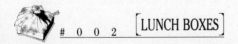 # 0 0 2 [LUNCH BOXES]

Do Ghouls do that? Do I?

Is it really just the boundary between Ghouls and humans that keeps me and Yoriko apart? Or have I actually been the one keeping us apart?

"Is there anything you could do for Yoriko that would make her happy?"

Kaneki's words came to Touka's mind. *Something simple that a human or a Ghoul could do. And I can't do that because . . . I'm the weak one?*

"Shit!" Touka yelled, and began to run toward Anteiku.

"Hey, you!"

As soon as Touka walked in the door, she shouted at Kaneki.

"Y-you could at least call me by name, Touka."

"Come with me after work!" Touka ordered Kaneki, interrupting him. Kaneki rolled his eyes, but despite Touka not explaining anything he must have sensed what it was about.

"Okay," he said in agreement.

"Boss, I'm sorry, but could we possibly finish a little early today?"

She was much more polite to Yoshimura when she asked than she had been to Kaneki. Like Kaneki, Yoshimura did not ask why, but smiled and said, "I'll let you this time, since you're always such a hard worker."

With Yoshimura's blessing, Touka and Kaneki left at a much

earlier time than usual. Kaneki followed behind Touka, who clearly had a destination in mind.

"Hey, Touka? Where are we going?" Kaneki asked, starting to get worried.

"Just shut up and follow me," Touka said. *He's only here because I asked him, so what's with the attitude?* Touka wondered to herself.

But Kaneki looked like he was used to it. "Got it," he said.

"This is where we're going?"

It was about fifteen minutes' walk from Anteiku. They had arrived at a supermarket—a place that held no importance for Ghouls. Touka went in. The smell of human food made her feel like she was going to throw up, but she ignored it and pushed forward.

She stopped in the middle of the supermarket and looked back at Kaneki.

"So what should I buy?"

"Huh? Why would you . . ."

"I need stuff to put in a lunch!"

Kaneki stared blankly at her for a second, then immediately began laughing.

"Don't laugh!"

"S-sorry! Okay, I get it, I understand."

She hadn't told him everything, but he still seemed to get the idea.

"We need something you can manage to eat that's also rich and luxurious. There's usually a few cooking magazines in the magazine racks at supermarkets, so maybe we should start there," he said,

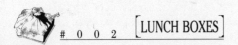

and started walking with the idea that Touka would follow. Kaneki looked authoritative then, if only a little.

————————

"Wow, guys, what's all this?"

Hinami, who had been waiting at home, was wide-eyed in surprise at the sight of Touka and Kaneki, their arms full of bags from the supermarket.

"I'm going out tomorrow so I'm making packed lunches."

"Lunches?"

"We're going to make great ones. Uh, Touka, we'd better make

what we can now. It might take a while, so maybe we should get started." Kaneki pushed up his sleeves and opened the cookbook they'd bought, checking the instructions and arranging the ingredients.

"Can I help you guys?" Hinami said, sounding enthused. Touka passed her some ingredients, along with a large lunch box she'd bought.

"Okay, can you wash this for me?" she asked. Hinami nodded emphatically and turned on the faucet.

"Let's start with the fried chicken."

Kaneki measured the spices out and mixed them in a bowl. He added the chicken and covered it in the seasoning. His movements were clumsy, but he seemed to be following the book's directions.

"Touka, can you get the potato starch ready for me?"

"Potato starch?"

"It's that stuff. You put it on a plate."

Touka, moving more clumsily than Kaneki, picked up the potato starch and nervously poured it out on a plate. She held the plate out to Kaneki, who grinned. He carefully took the chicken out of the marinade and rolled it in potato starch.

Watching Kaneki's profile as he cooked felt somehow nostalgic to Touka.

As Touka and Kaneki kept cooking despite being out of their element, the dishes came together one by one.

"I feel like we're doing pretty well at this."

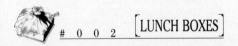 # 0 0 2 [LUNCH BOXES]

There were sandwiches, asparagus spears wrapped in bacon, an omelet, battered fish, and fried chicken.

The biggest difficulty was that they couldn't taste any of it. But with who knows what in mind, Kaneki picked up a piece of the chicken and popped it in his mouth.

"Wait!"

"Kaneki?!"

"Whoa!"

And he spat it out immediately.

"Gross!"

"Are you all right?!"

Kaneki wiped at his tongue with a tissue handed to him by Hinami.

"I thought it looked so good! But it was awful—the batter was like mulch that's been dragged through slime, and the meat was like chewing on a big, fat earthworm . . ." he groaned.

"Why on earth did you think it looked good?"

It was already past midnight, and the three of them had filled up the large lunch box with their cooking. Hinami rubbed her eyes occasionally out of sleepiness.

"I guess I was just remembering. Hah," Kaneki muttered, looking at the lunch they were putting together. Before Touka could ask what he'd remembered, she saw his face. He looked like he was yearning for something, but it was deeply tinged with sadness.

They sat in silence.

It wasn't so long ago that he had a very, very normal life as a human. Maybe this is the kind of lavish lunch he ate before it happened.

Who has it worse—someone who was never equipped with a function, or someone who had it and lost it?

Touka sighed, blowing air through her nose, and did not continue the conversation.

"There we go, all done!"

By the time everything was in place it was already one in the morning. Sleepiness had gotten the best of Hinami, who was asleep on the sofa.

"I'm sorry about earlier."

It was the kind of phrase that could have started it all over again, but Kaneki smiled and said, "It's all right." He paused. "In this book I just read . . ."

"Don't give me that. I want to hear what *you* think."

They got along well, but that was the one thing in their way. Kaneki scratched his head and changed tactics. "Okay, well, it's a line from a movie, but have you seen the movie *Giant*? It's an American movie about a Texas ranching family. One of the characters says, 'The best part about quarreling is making up.'"

Touka stared at him.

"I guess the movie's based on a novel by a female writer called Edna Ferber."

"And here we are back to books again!"

She gave him a kick instinctively, and Kaneki yelped in pain. But his expression softened and he spoke again.

"Hide and I used to fight over stupid stuff too. But we're still friends. I hope it goes well tomorrow."

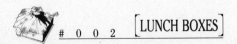 # 0 0 2 [LUNCH BOXES]

Thanks for the encouragement. With those words, Kaneki left Touka's house.

Touka lifted Hinami up from the sofa and carried her to bed. She listened to the sound of her breathing as she slept and smoothed her hair, then went back to the kitchen and looked at the finished lunch.

"God, that was a lot of work."

How many hours altogether did we spend on making this lunch? And people do this day after day, three meals a day?

Is this how much time Yoriko always puts into her cooking?

Touka put the lid on the lunch box and closed her eyes. *I can't tell her how I feel in words, so I hope I can get it across in this form . . .*

VI

"Looks like she's home."

At eight the next morning, Touka stood in front of Yoriko's house. There were signs someone was in, but Touka couldn't tell whether it was Yoriko or not. Nervously, she rang the doorbell.

"Helloooo . . . Touka?"

Yoriko's mother answered first. Judging by her very surprised tone, Yoriko had probably told her that the planned zoo trip was off. Touka quickly bowed her head.

"Is Yoriko in?" she asked.

"I'm sorry, but she's still asleep. Just a second, I'll go wake her up."

Yoriko's mom padded off. Not a moment later, she heard a voice say, "Touka's here?!" then a few minutes later, Yoriko appeared in her pajamas, combing through her hair with her hands.

"Touka?" she said, unable to hide her surprise. Touka said nothing and held out a bag to her.

"What's this?"

"Lunch." Yoriko looked up from the bag in surprise. Touka didn't know how she should look as she met Yoriko's eyes, but somehow she looked her straight in the eye.

"Let's go to the zoo," she managed to say. But unable to bear the emotion of the situation, she looked down. She waited for Yoriko to say something, but she gave absolutely no reply.

She'd thought that if she did something to make Yoriko happy then things would go back to normal, but perhaps it wasn't that simple. *Maybe I've made things worse*, she thought, quickly feeling embarrassed by her own selfish behavior.

When she looked up out of anxiety, Yoriko was also looking down. *Maybe things can't go back to the way they were before anymore.*

A drop fell onto Yoriko's cheek. The light in her eyes was the same that Touka had seen when, in her fury in the hallway at school, she'd wanted to fire back at Mayuhara.

"Yoriko . . ."

Her teardrops kept dropping, like rain just beginning to fall.

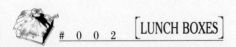

0 0 2 [LUNCH BOXES]

"I'm sorry."

Yoriko opened her mouth, breaking the silence.

"Mayuhara . . . told me all I did was annoy you, Touka. What if that's what I was doing, if I was just being too pushy? The idea scared me . . ."

Her hands tightly gripped the bag with the lunch in it as she started to open up to Touka about the feelings she had been burdened with.

"I wondered, what if you really did hate me? And I, I got scared, it scared me . . ."

The idea that she thought that far . . . Touka shook her head. *It's not true, absolutely not.*

"You're always so cool and collected, Touka—all the things that I'm not, the ideal girl, but . . . But I can't speak my mind to people like you can, and I'm dumb, and there are a lot of things I don't pick up on, and all I do is drag you down. I'm so useless . . ."

Don't think that. I'm so much more imperfect than you, and I make idiotic mistakes, and I'm oblivious to the pain of others because I'm too used to pain myself.

But you're not like that, Yoriko. I feel calmer just being around you—that's the kind of presence you have. You're so, so many of the things I'm not.

"I . . . had some suspicions about you, I guess. I kind of couldn't believe we were friends, even though we were. But then you were so nice to me, despite everything about me . . . I'm sorry. I'm so sorry, Touka. I'm sorry . . ."

So many emotions welled up in the pit of Touka's heart. There were so many things she wanted to say to Yoriko, but she couldn't get a single word out through the frustration and the pain. She opened her mouth to try to speak, then closed it without saying anything, before repeating the same action.

Say something, say something now!

Her irritation with herself took her even further away from being able to speak. *God, I just want to cry now.*

But it was then that Yoriko raised her head.

"Touka..."

She looked straight at Touka's face and, wiping her tears with the palm of her hand, she smiled.

Yoriko grabbed Touka's hand tightly.

"Oh... you never can hide your feelings, can you?"

It's okay, the message got across, Touka felt like she'd heard her say.

———————

"Look, Touka, there's a baby lion!"

Afterward, they went to the zoo together. Yoriko happily and excitedly ran ahead on her own. Touka chased after her.

In the petting zoo they found a rabbit, and Touka carefully reached out to try to touch it. But the rabbit slipped through her hands and got away. When she seemed sad about it, Yoriko picked the rabbit up in her arms and let Touka pet it.

"Wow, this looks great! Did you really make all of this?"

At lunchtime, they spread out a blanket on a grassy patch and opened their lunchboxes. Yoriko's eyes gleamed with surprise when she looked inside. Touka struggled for words for a moment before saying, "Sort of." Kaneki had made most of it, but it didn't really matter.

"I never knew you could cook like this, Touka... It's so delicious! And perfectly seasoned!" That was Kaneki's doing too.

"I won't be outdone!" Yoriko said, her eyes burning with competitiveness.

Touka laughed drily as she picked up a piece of chicken with her chopsticks and held it out to Yoriko.

"What?"

"Open up."

Touka tried giving a bite to her, like Yoriko always did. She seemed embarrassed to have it done to her, and she opened her mouth a little shyly.

Just then, they heard footsteps on the grass—someone was approaching.

Touka caught a snippet of their conversation.

"But nobody thought you'd be reassigned to the 20th Ward on an extraordinary basis, Yanagi."

"It was Rank 1 Investigator Mado's decision, so nobody can do anything about it."

Touka dropped the chicken from her chopsticks in surprise. But it landed perfectly in Yoriko's waiting mouth. Yoriko hadn't taken note of the men; she was busy chewing. Touka kept her body toward

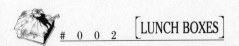 # 0 0 2 [LUNCH BOXES]

her friend, moving just her eyes to look at them. She saw two men with attaché cases staring right at her.

Ghoul investigators!

No way have I ever run into these guys in a place like this. But on second thought, they have to do patrol routes through the places where people go too. What if the suspicious person that Yoshimura was talking about was this Ghoul investigator, Mado's replacement?

If he realizes I'm the "Rabbit" this place'll be a battlefield in an instant. And right in front of Yoriko's eyes . . .

A chill ran down Touka's spine. Her heart started pounding. The investigators still had not taken their eyes off her.

"The fried chicken is so tender!" Yoriko said, her hand pressed to her cheek, breaking Touka's sudden tension. Involuntarily distracted by this, Touka was open to attack. *Dammit*, she thought, and focused all of her attention on where the investigators were.

"Doesn't this place just warm your heart?"

The investigators, however, were at ease.

"It's peace like this we're bound to protect. Ready to go, Toujou?"

"Yessir."

With that, they left.

Dumbfounded, Touka was watching the men leave in stunned silence when Yoriko broke in to ask, brightly, "So which do you think is your best creation?" To those men, Touka had looked like nothing but a happy schoolgirl sharing jokes with a friend.

"Well, I'd say . . . the chicken?" Touka said, smoothing all traces of the investigators from her heart as they walked into the distance.

"I knew you'd say that." Yoriko nodded, then laughed quietly as if she'd just thought of something.

While Touka wondered what it was, Yoriko picked up a piece of chicken and held it out to Touka.

"Your turn."

It was a scene just like always, part of their unchanging daily life. Although Touka was a Ghoul and couldn't stand human food, Yoriko's smile brought calm to her heart.

Touka took a bite of the chicken. As always, it was the worst thing she'd ever tasted, but Touka lifted the corners of her mouth and gave a faint smile.

"No, yours is."

"Mine is what?"

"The fried chicken you make is better."

Human relationships are full of lies. But that's also how Touka, by making an effort, was able to hold on to her own normality.

"Today was really fun," Yoriko murmured softly, reluctant to admit their day was over. They were in the train on the way back, and the sun was just beginning to set. Touka nodded, gazing at the red-tinged world out the window.

For a moment, at least, it feels like we've gone beyond the divide between humans and Ghouls, like we're sharing the same feeling.

0 0 2   [LUNCH BOXES]

[PHOTOS]

*L*et it be known to the world. I am Shu Tsukiyama, the Gourmet.

All of this happened a few years before Kaneki had that run-in with Rize. He was still going through his life as a human, still living under the delusion that the world was peaceful. But there were already Ghouls on the streets.

On a night the moon shone brightly, I had one prey I was targeting. My favorite part was the calves. This man, whose daily routine after work included preparing for a marathon, had apparently run the big one in Hakone in the past.

But he had no legs to run on anymore. He'd noticed someone suspicious behind him, and the sight of him trying to run as hard as he could was beautiful. But I'm a Ghoul—I'd chase after a baby if it was dinnertime.

"Muscles that dance across the earth... and perfect proportions, too. At this moment, I must give my thanks to you for continuing your healthy lifestyle so I could devour you!"

In the middle of the completely deserted park, the man who had lost both of his legs lay basking in a sea of his own blood, in shock and losing consciousness.

How sad that he didn't put up much of a fight. But in my hand I held his leg, which couldn't have stimulated my appetite any more.

"Don't worry, this is the main dish. And thanks for doing all the prep work for me. I think I should partake before you get near to death!"

Ecstasy flashed over Tsukiyama's face as he began to lick up the blood from the man's severed lower leg.

To be called a boy suggests that one's body is supple and still growing; to be called a youth suggests some innocence still remains. His eyes, red as a pomegranate, emphasized that he was something grotesque, though he exuded a bewitching charm.

Tsukiyama was sixteen years old.

When the sun reigned over the world, he worked hard at his studies just like any other "normal high schooler," but the truth was that he was a Ghoul.

It was a life he chose, the one he should have chosen. And then to make himself even better he had to be into gastronomy.

"May this meal make me even more radiant!"

Tsukiyama opened his mouth wide enough to distort his beautiful face, ready to sink his teeth into the man's powerful calf.

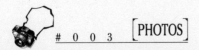

And that is precisely when it happened.

A dazzling flash, like a bolt of lightning. Then the loud snap of a camera shutter. Tearing off the man's flesh with his teeth, Tsukiyama looked around for the source of the light and sound. But before he could get his bearings, a voice boomed out unexpectedly.

"Allriiiiiight, got the photoooooooo!"

In one hand was a digital SLR camera; the other hand was held up to the starry sky. And below this raised fist was a girl—no more than twelve years old, judging by her appearance.

His attention was pulled away from his meal to the girl, the flesh he was eating passing down his throat half-chewed. The second he gulped Tsukiyama came back to his senses. He began to shake with anger.

"You interrupted me!"

He had barely tasted the dinner he'd gulped down. The girl bounced happily, like the pure embodiment of joy, with absolutely no clue what she'd done.

"That was my first bite too!"

Tsukiyama tossed aside the man's leg and kicked the ground. The impact was enough to leave a hole. He went straight at the girl, teeth bared and ready to take her life. *Add another body to the count*—or not.

"Agh!"

The girl stooped slightly, ducking behind something—the play-ground slide.

As Tsukiyama's fist destroyed one of the poles of the slide, the girl shouted, "Wow!" with an admiration suggesting she did not understand the seriousness of the situation, then ran away at full speed. The backpack she was wearing swung from side to side as she ran.

Who manages to escape from Shu Tsukiyama? Is she a Ghoul or an investigator? But she didn't smell like a Ghoul, and she didn't have a Quinque, those weapons the humans use against us. She smelled like a human—like any old human.

The girl ran off without any hesitation, as if she were familiar with the geography of the area. *She seems much faster than the guy who was meant to be my dinner.* Tsukiyama chased her as she ran down the narrow streets, blowing right past people's houses and making wild movements in every direction.

Tsukiyama used some boxes he happened to find outside a storefront as a platform to leap from, then grabbed on to the foothold spikes on a utility pole, swung back like a gymnast on the horizontal bar and leapt to the top of the building, all in one move.

"You little—! Get back here, you scampering devil of a mouse!"

This bizarre late-night chase through the slumbering streets, the thudding weight of their footsteps. Even if he couldn't see her he could sense her. *And then there's my exceptional sense of smell.*

Before long, the girl stopped in a narrow alley. The chase was over. Tsukiyama leapt down from the rooftop, landing a short distance from the girl.

The girl was sitting on the ground with her back to him, her little body moving slightly. *Looks like she's shaking with fear.*

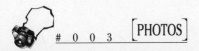
0 0 3 [PHOTOS]

Tsukiyama again observed the girl's appearance. She had a small frame and simply cut black hair. And she somehow resembled a hamster—although perhaps that was because she was sitting with her back hunched.

He looked at her in admiration, wondering how there could be a human that held so little fascination for him, with a body that provoked a surprising lack of his interest.

But the crime of interrupting Shu Tsukiyama while he was eating had consequences. How would he take out his anger? He started walking toward the girl as he pondered this.

"Ta-dah!"

But that's when the girl turned around. *She really doesn't get what she's in for.* Her joyful smile stood out in the darkness. He didn't know what she was thinking, and for a moment he was unsure of what to do.

Then the girl yelled proudly, "Look, they're really cool!"

She had a laptop open. *And all over the screen was—*

"Is that me?!"

—me, taking a bite of my prey's flesh.

"Oof," the girl said and stood up, then peered at his face.

"You're Shu Tsukiyama, aren't you?"

To his greater shock, she knew his name.

Who is this hamster?

The threat level of the girl he was face-to-face with suddenly skyrocketed. Tsukiyama was on guard.

The girl took something out of her backpack.

"Here, look!"

Without hesitation, she showed Tsukiyama a student ID from Seinan Gakuin University's high school, where he also went. The card had a photo of her face and the name Chie Hori on it.

"Chie . . . Hori?"

"You can call me Chiehori."

Chiehori put her student ID away and with a carefree smile she said, "God, all that running's got me wanting something sweet!"

It was late but they found a café that was open. Chiehori sat across from Tsukiyama, eating an extra-large parfait at top speed. *Her greediness, as if she has not eaten in days, is unbearably crass.*

"Can you not eat in a more ladylike fashion, you filthy little rodent?"

Tsukiyama snatched up his coffee cup in irritation. "Well, I'm not a lady," she shot back. Certainly, from her appearance she couldn't be any further from being a lady.

She finished up her parfait quickly and drank all of her juice. Then, finally, Chiehori started to talk. "I just knew I'd find something newsworthy about you!"

Newsworthy. Does that mean she's going to try to sell a story about me somewhere, or is she going to blackmail me?

She flicked through the photos on her camera. "So I just had to keep lying in wait. And then, bingo! Couldn't be happier," she said, blithely going on about her achievement.

Is she toying with me here? Tsukiyama set his coffee down on its saucer. "What are you aiming at?" he asked. Chiehori tilted her head.

"Aiming at? I already got it."

"*Excusez moi?*"

"I got it. See?" she said, shaking the camera up and down. "I was following you because I wanted to take some great photos. And they turned out better than I expected. So I got what I was aiming for."

"That's not all, though, is it? Getting the definitive scoop on me falls well outside the realm of a personal hobby!"

"Oh, do you want to be exposed? Because I can do that in a heartbeat."

Chiehori started taking her laptop out of her backpack.

"*Non, non* . . . Calm down now, my little friend."

"Oh, so which is it?" she grumbled. Nevertheless, she obediently set her backpack aside.

Still, how can she be so calm in front of me, a Ghoul, when she just saw me eating a human leg a little while ago? She nonchalantly took photos of what is, to a human, an inhumanly brutal, predatory scene.

What is it at the root of her mentality? Could she be some kind of extraordinary predator herself? Like the saying goes, a skilled hawk hides its talons. She was able to take a photograph of me at the most crucial moment without me noticing, so it's conceivable. I could understand easier if that were the case.

"Is it that the act of taking photos is something sublime for you? Enough that you don't care if you lose your life over it?" Tsukiyama asked her, taking a new approach. If you asked most humans about their passion in life, they would happily tell you all about it. *And maybe Ghouls aren't so different.*

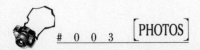 # 0 0 3 [PHOTOS]

"It's nothing that involved. I don't want to die over it."

Chiehori seemed like she'd lost interest in talking; she jiggled her leg up and down. She gave absolutely no indication that she'd eat him.

"I don't understand—so why did you do it?"

"Hm?"

Chiehori had a distant look on her eyes. For a while she was silent. *Fine, I'll wait.* However trivial her explanation, it would be a step toward understanding and uncovering the essence of her unconscious.

"Oh, I'm really sleepy now."

But her answer was rather disappointing. Chiehori stood up, rubbing her eyes with her hands and yawning uncouthly.

"Don't worry, I don't want to show the photos to anyone. I value my life too much for that. Thanks for the parfait. See you," she said. And with that she slung her backpack over her shoulders and turned briskly to walk off.

"Wait, you little rat!"

She did not listen to Tsukiyama's attempt to halt her, and in the end she pushed the check over to Tsukiyama and left the café.

"*Santo cielo*! Are you trying to test me here?"

Left on his own now, Tsukiyama ordered another coffee and lost himself in thought.

It would be easy to kill her. But it would be too rash to kill her without understanding nearly anything about her, and there is the possibility that this is some kind of trap to simply get me to bare my fangs and hit me with some unthinkable retaliation in return.

At the same time, a gentle voice echoed in Tsukiyama's mind.

"Tsukiyama, you ought to take a bit more care."

The voice belonged to the manager of Anteiku, Yoshimura. When he'd dropped into the café the other day, Yoshimura had given him those words of warning.

I told him then that I had no blind spots, that there was no need to worry about me.

"Mr. Yoshimura, were you talking about that little mouse?"

Because of this he couldn't make light of the danger. Tsukiyama tapped his fingernails against the coffee cup.

II

The prestigious high school was affiliated with Seinan Gakuin University. With an academic policy of respecting the independence and creativity of students, enhancing their value as individuals, and improving their capabilities, the school's selling point was not just its record of high test results—it was also a celebrity school, with many of its enrolled students coming from wealthy families.

"Good morning, Tsukiyama."

"You're looking very cheerful this morning."

"Oh, good morning, you charming girls. You sound just like angels today."

He had a beautiful way with words, and an elegant, pleasant

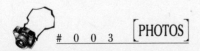

0 0 3 [PHOTOS]

way of speaking. Tsukiyama gave smiles to everyone, including the well-mannered girls who'd been pampered since birth.

"Charming . . ."

"I hear that a lot."

But because, unlike the elementary and middle schools affiliated with the university, the high school had many more students from the general population, there were more than a few ill-mannered students as well. Tsukiyama set his sights on the students gossiping in the back corner of the classroom.

"All I said was the same thing everyone thinks about those girls, though. I mean, don't get your feelings all hurt every time someone doesn't praise you from the bottom of their heart . . ."

If Tsukiyama narrowed his eyes as if to say, "You sure about that?" they would be pulled into the unique atmosphere that Tsukiyama had and sink into silence. The weak are no match for the strong, even when the strong don't show their claws.

"Oops, on another subject . . ."

Tsukiyama left the classroom and headed toward his next two classes. Since his person of interest was not at school yet, he propped himself up against the wall in the hallway, arms crossed, and waited for about ten minutes.

"Bingo."

The noisy clip-clop of footsteps reached Tsukiyama's ears. It was Chiehori, the girl who had caught him in the act on camera last night. She had her camera hanging around her neck, and her nonregulation backpack slung over her shoulders.

Tsukiyama stepped away from the wall and turned to face her. She took a moment to recognize him.

But all she said was, "Morning!" before going into the classroom. *Does this mean that what she said last night was true—that she got what she wanted and didn't want anything else to do with me?*

No, can't let my guard down yet. She knows my secret now, after all.

From that day on Tsukiyama regarded Chiehori with extreme caution.

"Oh, you mean Chie? I don't know how else to put it—she's a legendary weirdo. Even at this school."

Everyone he asked about her said the same thing: obsessed with photography, bizarrely unconcerned with social norms.

He had never noticed her before, but now that he had, he saw that she was restlessly energetic, always chasing after bugs in the courtyard during break or climbing a tree after school to take pictures of the sky.

"Chie's at it again."

"Where's she find the energy?"

As the whispered conversation reached his ears, Tsukiyama also heard Chiehori's footsteps. They beat out an unhesitant staccato. *How much energy does she have?*

"There you are."

Then Tsukiyama heard another set of footsteps approaching.

"Mr. Tsukiyama, may I have a word with you?"

His homeroom teacher, Ms. Matsumae, had just appeared in the

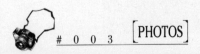

[PHOTOS]

classroom. It was break time. Tsukiyama said yes and stepped into the hallway.

"Shall I take care of her for you, sir?"

She said it quietly, so that nobody around them would hear. Tsukiyama shook his head quietly in admonishment.

"Matsumae... Thank you for caring about me, but this is my problem. If I can overcome this, I feel like I'll be able to apply what I learn to bigger problems too. I have to take care of this myself."

Matsumae was an employee of the Tsukiyama family. Naturally, she was also a Ghoul.

"Shu, sir, I was acting presumptuously out of too much concern for you. I am full of shame now."

"No, it's fine. You expressed your feelings well enough. There is something you could do for me, though—could you check into her for me?"

Matsumae nodded reverently.

"Yes, sir. Chie Hori is from a very normal, average family. Her

test results were good and she received a scholarship to attend this school, but since she was admitted her grades have been inconsistent, and at times this poses difficulties regarding her scholarship."

Seems she's not serious about studying. So then why'd she choose this school? Just as Tsukiyama wondered this, Matsumae added, with perfect timing, "The reason she gave for applying to this school is that it was the closest to her house. Anyway, she has since maintained her grades at the level needed to continue to receive her scholarship, but as you know, her only passion is photography. She's not in any clubs or on any teams, but the photography club advisor has seen her photographs, and she said that while some of Chie's pictures are as bad as if a child took them, some of them are almost miraculous and don't seem like they could have been taken by an amateur."

So just like with school, she's inconsistent when it comes to photography. Like a guinea pig skittering around without a purpose.

"I also teach her class sometimes, and my honest impression of her is that she is hard to pin down. She doesn't study hard enough to call her serious, and her behavior is not bad enough to call her unserious."

"It's hard to tell the difference between a fool and a wise man. Just like the zero card of the tarot deck, The Fool."

"I have not been very helpful. My apologies, sir."

"No, it's fine. If there's anything else, let me know."

"As you wish, sir."

It seemed like he would not be able to deal with this by ordinary means. Nonetheless, the more he looked into this girl he hadn't

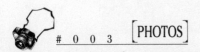

known at all until now, the more mysterious she became. *Perhaps I need to improve my understanding of people.*

Tsukiyama had gone back into the classroom and sat in his seat when the girl who sat next to him asked, "Did something happen?" She had silky, beautiful black hair and intellectual eyes. But within those eyes shone a dazzling glint of passion, contradicting first impressions.

"Miss Ikaru. Were you listening in?"

"You two were talking so loud it's more like you *made* me listen. What happened with Chie?"

An ordinary person could not have heard their whispering in the hallway from inside the classroom, filled with the buzz of break time. But as to whether she was a Ghoul, that was another story.

Ghouls lurk in everyday life. Ikaru was also excellent at fitting into human society. Some were remarkably good, having the right attitude and taking the effort needed to hide their identity and blend in with humans.

"What happened is, she took a picture of me while I was feeding."

"No way."

"Idiot me . . . Really."

Tsukiyama shrugged and shook his head in disbelief at himself. She frowned.

"Why haven't you killed her?"

"I haven't figured her out yet."

"Well, you're taking your sweet time about it," she murmured, sounding astonished. Just then, Chiehori came in from the hallway. The two of them observed her.

"I wasn't aware of her because I took no interest in her, but that little mouse is pretty famous at this school for being a weirdo."

"You're pretty famous here too, you know, for being the heir of the venerable, noble Tsukiyama family. For having great powers of influence due to strong friendships in the political and business worlds. It was your grandfather's generation that built up huge amounts of assets, wasn't it?"

"My grandfather was also an adventurer. He made his fortune by importing and exporting 'curiosities' from all over the world. I'm very proud of him," Tsukiyama said, putting his hand to his chest to show his respect.

"On top of that, you yourself are an accomplished student and your beauty is comparable to a model. And yet, your behavior is strange . . . bizarre. Terrible but eye-catching. And you and all of your family have, until now, been able to stand out without being caught. I can't help but admire you."

Just then, Chiehori dashed in from the hallway again. They stopped talking, and both of them turned their eyes toward her.

"But really, she's so animated that I can't believe you hadn't noticed her until now. I guess she didn't meet your standards."

Also, she had a monotonous, uninteresting smell, like the part of your index finger that never moves, and an utterly charmless, childlike body type. He must've unconsciously excluded her from his list of gastronomic interests.

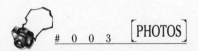

"Still, it's strange, isn't it? She has no financial means to speak of, but still she has a good camera with a high-spec lens. That's top-of-the-line."

Tsukiyama was unfamiliar with the financial limitations of common people, but he assumed that kind of gear would be too expensive a gift for her parents to give. She didn't seem to have an after-school job. *How did she get her hands on that camera?*

"Apparently she uploads her pictures to the internet as stock photos."

"Stock photos?"

"Yeah. Like you get money if they're used for commercial purposes. But primary-source photos have an even higher value."

Did she really have the knowledge to do that? Tsukiyama found himself becoming interested in a girl he had been indifferent to, little by little. But he couldn't forget she was the girl who knew his secret.

And now, is the game afoot?

Watching as Chiehori ran out into the hallway for the third time, Tsukiyama's smile intensified.

After school that day, he found her belly-crawling across the school lawn. He approached and tried to see just what on earth she was looking at, but he saw nothing but grass. Only the clicking of her camera shutter going off could be heard.

"What are you shooting, little mouse?"

"I found one."

Chiehori turned toward Tsukiyama and stood up like a shot.

"Check it out," she said. She fiddled with the camera, then showed him the picture she'd taken.

"I beg your pardon, but all I can see is the grass."

"Well, yeah. The picture's of the grass."

"Why? Grass is so boring."

It was hard to reconcile the idea that the same girl could take shocking pictures of a Ghoul midfeast and also take pictures of some entirely uninteresting grass. The difference couldn't have been starker. But Chiehori seemed content.

I shouldn't have said that.

"Wait, now that I really look at it, it's not bad. Every blade of grass is bathed in a prism of light, and each one has this emerald glow . . . It's really interesting."

I can't afford to offend her now, Tsukiyama thought as he retracted his previous statement and praised her.

"Oh, really? I think it's boring, personally," Chiehori said. *God, this girl just does not behave how I expect.*

"My apologies," Tsukiyama said, breaking the silence. "Actually, there's somewhere I'd like to take you now. Don't worry, I'm not going to hurt you."

Tsukiyama searched her face discreetly as he spoke the words carefully. *She is a slippery one, but this is my chance to get her.*

"It's somewhere I'm sure you'll like—"

"Great," she answered readily, before he'd even put the bait on the hook. Tsukiyama was slightly taken aback. She fumbled with her camera.

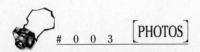 # 0 0 3 [PHOTOS]

"Sounds fun."

Perhaps her "sense of smell" is sharper than I thought.

III

He took Chiehori to the college hospital not far from the school.

"What's wrong, Tsukiyama?"

Chiehori raced around the grounds of the hospital without a pause, taking pictures of the building's exterior and the landscaping. Tsukiyama started speaking.

"There's something I want to tell you first," he said. "It's that I really like humans."

"So much that you eat them."

"Even if that's not my aim, is what I mean. People live their lives without claws or fangs, but still, humans have prospered on the earth. What drives them, I wonder—and what's at the heart of it?"

"But then you eat people."

"*Even though* I eat people."

The two of them entered the hospital, got on the elevator, and selected the floor for the general ward.

"Are you sure we can just waltz into the hospital like this?" Chiehori asked nonchalantly. The two of them were alone in the elevator.

"Oh, it's fine. I've taken everything into account."

They arrived at the eighth floor. On that floor there was an atrium as well as the ward. In this restful space, covered with grass and dotted with verdant trees, patients at the hospital and their families sat chatting in a peaceful atmosphere.

"Here we are," Tsukiyama said, casting a glance at the nurses' station. There were several nurses on duty behind the desk, and of those, one young female nurse had noticed Tsukiyama and Chiehori and was heading over to them.

"Oh, Tsukiyama, you came back? And you brought . . . Oh, I see, you go to Seinan, too," the nurse said, unable to hide a smile befitting such an angel in a white uniform. She seemed surprised that Chiehori, who looked nothing like a high school student, was wearing a Seinan uniform.

"This is my friend," Tsukiyama said.

"We're friends now?"

"When you share a secret with someone, that makes you friends," said Tsukiyama.

"Sounds suspicious if you ask me," teased the nurse. She didn't seem to really mean it. After all, the two of them were quite a mismatch.

Next, Tsukiyama introduced her to Chiehori.

"There's a lot of greenery at this hospital, as you can see. It's a pleasant place, so I was sitting on a bench on the grounds reading when she came over to talk to me. She has a very kind, polite manner, and she's very popular with the patients. And as you can see, she never can hide her beautiful smile either."

"Oh no, don't exaggerate." The nurse blushed with embarrassment. But Tsukiyama turned to her and continued.

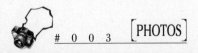

"It's just . . . love can be so painful."

"E-excuse me?!"

Tsukiyama clasped his hands to his chest and shook his head exaggeratedly, as if he were suffering over an impossible love.

"The doctor I'm in love with hardly looks my way. But if I got the chance I know we'd hit it off," he imitated her. Then he said, "There's not a man alive who wouldn't fall for your smile."

The nurse became flustered at having her innermost thoughts exposed, but she gave a wry smile at his last statement. "I hope so," she said.

Just then, someone appeared behind her.

"Chatting away with a young man, I see!" boomed a loud voice. It belonged to a male patient who seemed to be over ninety. He had emerged from his room behind them. His face was etched with countless wrinkles and his hairline was receding. He embraced the nurse from behind.

"Aah! Don't do that ever again!" she warned, turning around to face the patient clinging to her.

"Hm?"

At that moment, for some reason, Chiehori clicked the shutter.

I get it.

The old man let go of her and headed back toward his room with a grin on his face. With a pained smile, the nurse said, "I'm going to see him back to his room. Goodbye," and went off. As the two of them watched her go, Tsukiyama gave Chiehori an explanation.

"That old man has been hospitalized for a heart condition,

but sometimes he wanders off or does things like that, harassing the young nurses. And he forgets what he's done right away, so he doesn't feel any sense of shame."

But he also forgets the kindnesses people do for him. Forgetfulness is always with him.

"But he's a wealthy man, and he has relatives who are professors who work in this university hospital, so no one can say much to him."

Chiehori had her head down, checking her digital camera's display, and had not heard a word of Tsukiyama's story. She did everything at her own pace, and he couldn't hate her for it.

Tsukiyama leaned over and whispered in her ear.

"I'd like to invite you to a dinner theater tomorrow night."

She reacted with surprise and looked up at him.

"But you'll have to get the tickets yourself. Tomorrow night, around midnight, I'm going to sneak into that old man's room. I'll leave the window open for you. You should be able to get some marvelous photos."

This was the bait. He wanted her to imagine what might happen all she liked. And then he wanted her little chest to pound with excitement.

He waited for her answer. Finally, she let the camera go and nodded. "Got it," she said.

Should be a fun dinner.

Tsukiyama's lips curled into a smile.

IV

At seven thirty, when the sun had set, Chiehori went to the college hospital alone. It was the day she'd promised to meet Tsukiyama.

She'd come much earlier than they'd agreed, but with reason. Common sense said it would be impossible to sneak into a hospital at midnight. The doors would be locked and security would be there. So she pretended to be visiting a patient and entered the hospital first.

Right away she headed for the women's restroom. Once she was inside the stall, she took a pair of pajamas out of her backpack and changed into them. She stuffed the clothes she had been wearing into her bag, put her camera around her neck, and pressed the shutter button.

Now to find somewhere to stash my bag. Chiehori headed toward the hospital's courtyard. There she found a row of azalea trees along a path. Staying out of the lights nearby, she put her backpack behind one of the trees that the light didn't reach. She walked a few steps away to check. Her bag was nicely hidden and not visible thanks to the darkness.

"Oh."

Just then, she heard the chimes of the hospital's intercom system.

"This is an announcement for all visitors. Hospital visiting hours will be over shortly . . ."

Visiting hours ended at eight. People who had come to visit patients and had heard the announcement began to stream out of the hospital. A large number of patients stood at the door to see off their friends and family members.

Chiehori stood by the door for a while, idly watching the spectacle. She couldn't help imagining that everyone thought she was sad because her parents had gone home, since she looked no older than a middle schooler.

"Visiting hours are now over."

Shortly after the final announcement, the doors were locked. Chiehori slipped into the crowd of patients returning to their rooms and went into the hospital. There were over a thousand patients at this hospital. But there was also a high turnover of patients, and there was no way that staff would remember every one of them.

As she walked in she passed by doctors and nurses, but none of them, seeing her walk with such confidence, had the slightest suspicion.

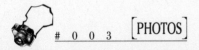

0 0 3 [PHOTOS]

"Well, here we go."

She arrived at the general ward on the eighth floor. From here on, she was out of her element.

Unlike outpatient doctors and nurses, ward nurses would know most of the patients on the floor they were responsible for. What's more, most of the patients in the ward were elderly. Someone with the appearance of a child wandering around the ward would stand out and be noticed without a doubt.

Chiehori went into the restroom again so as not to be spotted by the night shift nurse. Then she put the toilet seat down, had a seat, and waited for a while. The ward was still noisy, and she could hear the sound of people's footsteps. Occasionally a patient came into the bathroom, but there were enough stalls available that nobody minded that one had been in use for a long time.

She passed the time by flicking through the pictures she had taken on her camera. There were the pictures she'd taken the day before at the hospital, as well as the ones of Tsukiyama eating someone.

"Whoa."

Has it been close to an hour yet? Classical music began to play over the speakers on the ward. Chiehori looked up.

She checked the time. It was nine o'clock, lights out.

The song finished, and the lights on the ward went out one by one. The light in the hallway facing the bathroom Chiehori was in went out as well. There was almost no sign of anyone.

She decided to stay in the bathroom for a while longer, finally emerging half an hour later. Treading lightly, she looked into the hall-way and saw no one there. Some small lamps were still on in rooms here and there, where the patients must have still been awake. She took off her shoes and carried them in her hands so as not to make a sound as she walked down the hallway.

The nurses' station was in the middle of the floor. She took a quick peek and saw two or three nurses behind the desk. In order not to be seen she ducked down and passed by slowly. The nurses on the night shift had their hands full, and they did not notice Chiehori at all.

"Here it is."

Finally she had made it to a private room in a corner of the floor. It was the room of the old man she had seen yesterday. She put her ear to the door to listen to what was going on and heard loud, persistent snoring. Quietly, Chiehori slid the door open.

As she did, a soft, sweet smell reached her from inside. The smell was rather strong. *Is that perfume?* With the lights off it was hard for her to get a feel for the room. Once inside, she proceeded with more caution than ever before.

"Oh, he's sleeping."

The curtains were drawn, and there was a large bed next to the window. In that bed slept the old man who had sexually harassed the nurse the day before. She waved her hand in front of his eyes. The old man did not notice.

"Hello in there . . ." she said quietly. The old man still did not wake up, so next she tried gently poking his cheek.

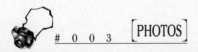
0 0 3 [PHOTOS]

"He's not waking up."

He seemed to be in a very deep sleep. *Maybe he's on sleeping pills. If so he simply won't wake up.* Chiehori's tension eased and she looked around the room anew.

"Wowww."

Could you even call this a hospital room? The interior was spacious and equipped with not just its own toilet, but also a shower. There was also a sofa and table, as well as a refrigerator, making it nicer than many hotel rooms.

She sat on the sofa and looked at the old man. *He must be as rich as Tsukiyama said if he has a private room this nice.* On the shelf, as if it were a display of power, were all kinds of gorgeous flowers, boxes of candy, and fruit baskets—probably gifts.

She stood up and looked at the fruit on the shelf. It seemed to be the source of the sweet smell filling the room. She picked up a mango, probably the most expensive thing there. The fragrant smell became even more intense. Wondering why, she turned it over in her hands and found that the other side was damaged and discolored.

"Hmm..."

No matter how many visitors brought gifts to him, there was likely nobody to help the old man eat what he was brought. It didn't look like the fruit knife sitting nearby had been used at all. Chiehori sat back down on the sofa and looked at the pictures she had taken of the old man the day before.

"Must be time soon."

She checked her watch. It was 11:55, not long before the time she'd agreed upon with Tsukiyama. Chiehori stretched her back and lay on the sofa on her side. Moonlight was coming in through a gap in the curtain.

Suddenly, she heard footsteps in the hallway. Her eyes popped open and she listened carefully.

The footsteps went down the quiet hallway, entered a room, went back into the hallway, and entered another room repeatedly. It sounded like a nurse doing the rounds.

That means someone's going to come in here, where I am.

She hesitated.

Chiehori looked around the room for somewhere to hide. She debated if it was acceptable to hide in the bathroom or shower. But the nurse's footsteps kept coming closer.

"Gotta do what you gotta do."

Taking advantage of her small body, she dove under the bed. A few seconds later, the door opened and a flashlight illuminated the room. *If it is the nurse doing her rounds she'll check on the man and then leave quickly.* To her surprise, though, the nurse closed the door and moved, not toward the bed where the old man slept, but in the direction of the shelves. And stayed there.

What on earth is she doing?

As Chiehori wondered this, she heard the sound of paper rustling. Then she heard the sound of someone chewing something.

It's the candy.

This nurse seemingly felt free to eat her patients' gifts. She went to the old man's bedside as she ate his sweets. Chiehori could see the

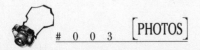

nurse's shoes from where she was hiding under the bed. They were cute, professional shoes, and somehow feminine.

Then there was a knock at the door. *I bet she's still got crumbs all over her hands*, Chiehori thought.

"Still kicking in there?"

Chiehori heard another sound, different from the one she'd heard before. It was the sound of something heavy hitting against something.

"Look, I can't move on to the next room until I get a reaction to confirm he's still alive."

Her voice was cold and haughty. Chiehori heard that heavy sound again.

She's hitting the old man, Chiehori guessed.

The old man groaned in pain. But the nurse did not stop.

"Looks like you're still with us. Ugh. What's the point? You'd be better off dead. Everybody thinks so too. What are you living for? It's disgusting. Just die, please, for everyone's sake, just die," the nurse spat out at the old man. But Chiehori's reaction was more to the voice than to the content. It was a voice she'd heard before.

The room echoed with the sound of her hitting the old man. Then she heard a huge crash.

"An angel in a white uniform indeed." The voice, a man's voice, belonged to Tsukiyama.

"W-what? Who's there?"

Surprised by the sudden intruder, the nurse tripped over her own feet and fell. Chiehori, hiding under the bed, saw her face then.

It was the nurse from the day before.

"Oh, why are you—Tsukiyama? Wait a minute, this is the eighth floor!"

"My apologies, I seem to have broken the window. I told her I'd open the window but my little mouse seems to have been fickle."

Tsukiyama jumped down into the room lightly. Chiehori also crawled out from under the bed.

"Oh, you're the girl who was with him yesterday . . . What is all this? Why are you here?"

"I'm sorry," he said. "So, little mouse, why don't you tell me all about it—the way she does her work? She's always doing this night after night, heaping abuse on patients she doesn't like."

Tsukiyama pointed at the nurse as if he were pointing her out to Chiehori. The nurse didn't seem to grasp the situation very well, but she seemed to understand that this was turning into the worst possible situation for her. She began to shake with fear.

Keeping his eyes on the nurse, Tsukiyama pulled the covers off the bed, exposing the old man's body where he lay.

"He has signs of internal hemorrhaging."

The nurse shuddered.

"But like how he forgets what he's done, he also forgets what others do to him. He has no idea how he gets hurt—he can't remember. So everyone thinks it's his fault, that he's hurt himself somehow, and nobody takes the matter any further. What a great storyline— I mean, really splendid, bravo!"

Tsukiyama turned to the nurse and applauded. After the final

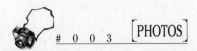

0 0 3 [PHOTOS]

clap, when his hands stopped moving, he slowly opened them and then picked up the part of the man's body that showed internal hemorrhaging with his fingertips. Tsukiyama gave a first-class smile.

"Well, now, it's dinnertime."

There was a ripping sound in the room, the sound of something being torn. Between Tsukiyama's fingers was the old man's skin.

The nurse screamed in spasmodic fear.

"The skin of the elderly is a delicacy, I've been told. It has a unique smell and texture that's very addictive to some."

Tsukiyama slowly lowered the old man's skin onto his tongue. To better savor the taste, he closed his eyes and brought it into his mouth as if he were licking it, rolling his tongue slowly. Then, he

chewed with consideration. Once he had swallowed, he opened his eyes wide.

"The conflicting tactile sensations of the nicely dry and rough skin and its reverse side, smooth and slick with blood, paired with the unique astringency that buzzes on the tongue all come together in an incredible harmonyyyyyy!"

He opened his arms wide and twisted his body toward the heavens. His eyes were dark, dark crimson.

"N-n-n-no way . . ."

His red eyes—his kakugan—blazed.

"Wh . . . what happened? I'm hurt, I'm hurt!"

Just then the old man, lying on his side on the bed, opened his eyes. The pain had finally broken through to his mind. Tsukiyama licked his lips and turned to the old man gleefully.

"Men have a shorter average life span than women, and there are especially few men in their nineties around. Men of your vintage are very rare!"

Again, Tsukiyama pinched the man's skin. And then he tore it off.

He screamed in agony.

"The flaky texture of the skin is just like powder! A most exquisite delicacy!"

"Stop, please stop . . ." the old man stuttered out.

"It's so nice to eat because it comes off so easily! And the process really enhances the experience!"

Tsukiyama was now rapidly tearing off chunks of the man's

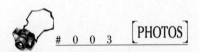

skin. The nurse could not move an inch. Somehow she managed to squeeze out a few words, her voice quivering.

"Tsukiyama, you're . . . you're a . . . Ghoul?"

He gulped down a piece of skin before answering.

"Heh, I'm a gourmet! I seek out the ultimate in eating experiences!"

In his panic the old man rolled away and fell out of the bed. He tried to crawl on his hands and knees across the floor, reaching out for the nurse.

"H-help! Help me!"

Tsukiyama had picked off the skin on his outstretched hand, and his sinewy muscles were visible.

"Help me, I'll do whatever you want, or give you whatever you want. I've got money, I've got land . . . Please, I beg you . . ."

The old man begged in hope of salvation, tears spilling to the ground. His thin arms were like dead trees. His hand struggled into the nurse's line of sight.

The nurse swallowed hard and gritted her teeth.

"Go away, old geezer!"

With all of her might, she kicked the old man where he lay on the floor.

At that moment, a light went off in the darkened room. And what illuminated the room was a camera flash. The shutter sound was alien and out of place in those surroundings.

Chiehori had captured the moment that the nurse had kicked the old man.

"So eccentric! You fascinate me endlessly!" Tsukiyama gave

Chiehori a few words of praise as he reached a hand out to her. Then he grabbed her by the collar of her pajamas and easily lifted her up to his eye level.

"No matter how much someone's suffering you don't take note, you little superiority-complex case! I can't hate you for it. What I think is, humans have been able to thrive for so long because of your tenacity in life, to put on a mask and become someone else for your own sake—it's in that cruelty that allows you to easily betray others! But . . ."

Tsukiyama smiled at her.

"But now the game's over!" he said, sticking Chiehori's body out the window. If he let go, she would tumble headlong toward the ground. And a certain death.

The wind was blowing along the building, and the curtains flapped. A temporary silence fell over the chaotic hospital room.

"Now tell me. Do you know what I can see in your eyes?"

Hiding a gleeful smile, he spoke to her as if all was exposed, as if he could see right through her. As he spoke, he lifted one finger of the hand that had hold of her.

"Seething fear, a rising sense of despair. The world losing its color, your heart frozen . . ."

Chiehori's feet flailed as if she was having trouble breathing, and her body shook slightly in reaction.

The choices she could make were limited now. She could become violent in a desperate attempt to escape, or she could start pathetically pleading for her life—those were her options.

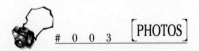

0 0 3 [PHOTOS]

At any rate, instead of holding herself aloof from the world still, she must now finally have inside her a rough sketch entitled "Emotion."

Tsukiyama lifted another finger away from her.

So, what kind of person are you?

If he let go it would not be long before she was knocking on the gates of the afterlife. Tsukiyama waited for her to say something.

But she did not utter a single peep. She looked up at the sky all of a sudden, then brought her gaze back to Tsukiyama and took her camera in hand.

Then, after looking at Tsukiyama through the viewfinder, she pressed the button.

"Mmm . . . good shot."

She made it clear to him that, even at the moment of her impending death, she would take pictures as always. That truth made Tsukiyama's skin crawl.

She was not so devoid of personality that she didn't care about sacrificing everything. To her, everything living existed in the same field. With a sense of values that went beyond the moral, she looked at all living beings equally. She saw no distinction between humans and Ghouls, dogs and cats, even between birds and fish—they were all the same to her. So she took things as they were, let her own curiosity run wild, and kept on taking the kind of photos that excited her. Her approach was instinctual and pure, nothing more.

Her mentality's not too different from mine—with my insatiable desire to keep searching for the greatest gastronomic experiences.

"Well, isn't this funny!"

Tsukiyama tightened his grasp on her clothing and pulled her back into the room.

"Easy does it."

Chiehori collapsed to the floor, her own sense of equilibrium thrown off by dangling in the air. But soon she picked herself up and stood on her own two feet.

She was silent for a second. "Oh, I'm alive. Lucky," she said.

Although she had just had a close call with death, the tone of her voice was light, rejoicing in her survival. Tsukiyama had a sudden realization.

"Oh, I get it now! You're like a pet!"

He was pleased at having found the answer. A puzzled expression crossed Chiehori's face.

"I couldn't figure out why you wouldn't lift a finger no matter what, but if I consider you the same as a pet it all makes sense! From now on, little mouse, I'm going to make you my pet!"

"What? No, I don't wanna be," Chiehori said plainly and started looking at the photos she had taken.

"Is this the same fascination humans have with cuddly cats? It's really intriguing!"

Without much consideration Tsukiyama patted Chiehori on the head. He looked at her and thought she'd be handy in size and easy to keep as a pet.

"Forget about that, Tsukiyama. Have you heard of scheduling blog posts?"

Chiehori put her camera down and looked up at Tsukiyama. It was a sudden change in topic.

"Of course. You write a post and then you have the ability to set a time you want it to go live. Right?"

"Exactly. The thing is, I scheduled a post with the photos I took of you eating to go up at exactly 1:00 a.m."

On the one hand, this meant that she had wanted to expose the brutal photos proving he was a Ghoul on the Internet. But she didn't seem to be trying to threaten Tsukiyama or deceive him, either.

"I set it up because I thought there was a chance I might die and my body would never be found, and I hated that idea. So I wrote something like, 'The culprit is Shu Tsukiyama, a student at Seinan Gakuin University High School, please investigate him.' But it seems like I've survived, so I've gotta delete that scheduled post."

She seems so useless, but she's logical; she seems so stupid, but she's very sharp.

Chiehori looked out the window from which she had nearly just been dropped, and pointed to an azalea tree a short distance away, where she had hidden her bag.

"Oh, but first we have to get out of here somehow. We can't just go strolling out of this hospital."

She rubbed her index finger against her temple, as if she had not thought that far ahead. Tsukiyama laughed out loud at the sight.

She does all these things uncalculatedly, as if they were natural to her. There's no category for her, she's just a unique creature called Chie Hori.

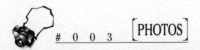 # 0 0 3 [PHOTOS]

"Well then, shall we leave this place?"

I got what I wanted. There's no use in being here anymore.

"Oh?"

Tsukiyama picked Chiehori up under her arms and stepped up onto the window frame. Then he turned back to look at the nurse, who stood on the other side of the hysterical old man. She was crouched down, trying to catch her breath.

He gave her a smile.

"I hope we can be good 'friends' with you, madam."

She made a confused sound, not understanding his meaning. Tsukiyama said nothing more before springing out the window.

"What on earth . . . What just happened?"

The menace threatening their lives had left. But the nurse's trembling still had not stopped, and she stayed sitting on the floor. She was too upset to move.

The first one of them to stand was the old man, who had been groveling on the floor. But soon he fell again, crying out in pain. The nurse looked at the old man's ungainly form and felt somewhat calmer. She put her hand against the wall for support and slowly stood up. Whatever else, she now had to go back to the nurses' station and report a Ghoul attack. She put her hand on the knob of the room's door.

"I won't forget . . ."

The old man's voice sounded like he had been crawling across the desert. The nurse looked at him in surprise.

"Everything you did to me, I won't forget it!"

He was bleeding from everywhere his skin had been torn off, but the old man shot a sharp eye at the nurse, stopping her in her tracks.

"I'm going to reveal everything, how you kept on hitting me! You wouldn't know humanity if it looked you in the eye, girl!"

Suddenly there was a crack, the sound of something breaking. Something that had been worn down under extreme circumstances.

The nurse's hand dropped from the doorknob. Silently, she walked back toward the old man.

She walked past where the old man was, then took a pair of gloves out of the pocket of her white coat.

She stopped in front of the shelves. She picked up the fruit knife from where it sat near the fruit, still giving off a sweet smell.

"W. . . what are you . . ."

The nurse turned back to the old man.

The edge of the knife gleamed in the sliver of moonlight that shone into the room.

V

A few weeks later, Tsukiyama was having a coffee after class at a café near the school. Sitting across from him, Chiehori was gobbling down a crepe.

"Oh, by the way, did you see what happened?"

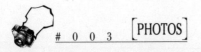
0 0 3 [PHOTOS]

Now feeling full, Chiehori opened her laptop and tapped at the keyboard. Then she turned it toward Tsukiyama to show him.

It was an article with the shocking headline, "Sickbed Bloodbath: Horror at the Hospital." The victim was a 94-year-old male patient.

With the amount of skin he'd had ripped off, the old man should have been able to survive if given immediate care. But the article used words like "murder" and "death."

"It looks like they're putting all the blame on me. But I feel sad for him."

The article said that a nurse on the night shift doing her rounds had tried to protect the patient from a Ghoul but was attacked herself, and fainted.

Chiehori turned the laptop back toward herself. "It was kind of your fault to begin with," she said.

"She'd been hiding her cruelty since the beginning. I just picked up on it."

Sparked by Tsukiyama's words, Chiehori started going back through the data on her camera, and looked again at the picture of the old man embracing the nurse.

She saw the nurse, the one who'd been referred to as unable to hide her smile, looking at the old man as if he were lower than a dog.

"Oh, this is it. I did meet that nurse before."

"Some hobby you have."

She had taken a picture of the nurse's decisive moment. Although in some situations there was a possibility of harm to herself, Chiehori crossed that particular dangerous bridge with typical calm.

"After all, she's now 'the brave nurse,' so she's getting a lot of sympathy at the hospital."

"Huh?"

"She told me, 'I'm going out with that doctor I always had a crush on now, thanks to you.' She expressed her gratitude to you, Tsukiyama. She said you're like a god."

The world is cruel. Just as doing good is not limited to helping people, doing wrong is not just about stealing someone's happiness. But that's what makes it interesting.

"Nobody's as powerful as a tragic princess."

Tsukiyama brought his coffee up to his lips and took a sip, rolling it over his tongue.

"I can't wait until her happiness gets flambéed," he said.

But it wouldn't be enough, not nearly enough.

Tsukiyama's own tongue was begging for it. The sublime taste that would send him into a daze—the taste of her happiness.

Someday I'll run into her again, I can feel it in my bones. Tsukiyama's smile deepened.

Chiehori saw, got him in her viewfinder, and pressed the button.

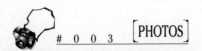

[**THE BIG CITY**]

*W*ith dreams in my head and my instrument on my back I go to the city. Let this sound someday reach the world.

"Okay, I'm heading off now."

The Shinkansen platform, just before departure. A young man stood with his beloved guitar slung on his back and huge suitcases in both hands. His friends who had come to see him off patted him on the shoulder and wished him good luck.

Momochi Ikuma, 22 years old. An aspiring musician moving to Tokyo.

"Mom?" Ikuma called to his mother, who was standing at a slight remove with a sad expression on her face. But she did not take a step toward him. Ikuma walked over to her.

"I'm gonna do my best, so don't worry," he said.

The bell signaling that the train was about to depart began to chirp. Ikuma got on board in a hurry. The doors closed, and the Shinkansen slowly pulled away.

"We're all behind you!"

"Good luck!"

His friends yelled out words of encouragement from the platform. His mother waved goodbye with tears in her eyes. And for Ikuma, the platform became smaller and smaller as the town he had been so used to living in suddenly got far away.

Ikuma thought about his friends and the look on his mother's face, and he cried alone.

Momochi Ikuma was a Ghoul.

"Wow, amazing..."

When he arrived in Tokyo, Ikuma was overwhelmed by the number of people everywhere. Occasionally he had come to Tokyo to go to concerts, but this dwarfed all those times.

All that seemed far away now that he was, from today on, living in Tokyo.

Ikuma gave himself a quick slap on the cheek to get motivated, then he excitedly boarded his next train.

It was true outside of Tokyo, too, but generally it seemed to Ikuma that a rough sort of people gathered here. And the same was true for Ghouls too. Tokyo was right in the middle of the country. The Ghoul population was huge, so something unexpected could happen at any moment. Tokyo was also the home of the CCG, professional Ghoul killers. Too bad if you got caught up by them.

0 0 4 [THE BIG CITY]

"All right, finally here."

Ikuma had chosen to live in the relatively peaceful 20th Ward, not too far from the heart of the city. There was lots of green space, even some fields here and there—it looked a little like his hometown.

And it was in the same neighborhood as Kamii University, so lots of other people his age lived there, making for good camouflage.

But the house was a tiny sliver of a place, which he couldn't get over. It was much smaller than his parents' house, but the rent was insanely high. Still, from now on this was his castle. First he had to buckle down to be able to pay the rent and utilities.

Ikuma took his guitar out of its case. It had been his closest

companion since he bought it in high school with money from his part-time job. He stretched his hands and started playing a song by his favorite band.

"Hey, shut it!" His neighbor banged on the wall and yelled at him to stop, so Ikuma quit playing quickly and apologized sheepishly through the wall. He checked his watch. It was 11:00 p.m.

Fair enough, he thought. *Welcome to the city, huh?*

And this is how Ikuma's Tokyo debut came to an end on his first day.

The next day Ikuma got a magazine of job listings and looked for something part time. He decided to go with a job as a mover. After all, he was a Ghoul and thus had several times the strength of a human.

There was just one more thing that Ikuma definitely had to do in order to continue living. That was securing some "food."

Sure, he had the "lunch box" that his mother had given him, but someday that would run out. Now that he was living on his own away from home, he would have to be able to get food on his own.

Ikuma changed into some black clothes that wouldn't stand out, got on the cheap bike he'd bought at a secondhand store, and set out into the darkening streets of the city.

"Whew, made it."

He had finally arrived at a famous suicide spot on a well-known hill. It was nearly two, so it was already pitch-black, and nobody was around.

He had a good view from where he stood, and he could see a sea of trees for about twenty meters down the hill. Ikuma sniffed hard, smelling for something.

"Really, nothing?"

He had thought this would be an easy place to find a corpse, but no scent of blood or death came to his nose.

But he couldn't just give up that easily.

After that night, Ikuma headed for the hill after work every day. With a four-hour round-trip it was quite hard work, but he used the time to work on his lyrics and come up with melodies in his head, and it wasn't that hard if he sang to himself.

"Hey, sorry, excuse me . . ."

But day after day he was faced with nothing but disappointment. Days went by wasted. Before he realized it, he had been in Tokyo for over a month.

"Oh, this isn't good . . ."

The "lunch box" his mother had given him was completely empty, and so was the refrigerator. Ikuma dragged himself outside sluggishly.

Better change it up. But what if I change location and run into someone? Oh God . . . he thought to himself.

He decided to ride to his usual hill that day anyway. As he neared the hillside, he was just thinking that he'd better come up with somewhere else to go if he struck out again that night when it happened.

The wind gently caressed his cheek as Ikuma suddenly hit the brakes on his bike.

"That smell . . ."

It was the smell of death.

Ikuma started pedaling with all his might. The bike tenaciously climbed the hill, but it was too slow for Ikuma.

"Here!"

Ikuma left his bike on the side of the road and ran off with all the force in his body. His eyes turned red at once, and his limbs had the power to act in response. It was his true nature, sleeping inside him until now. He kicked the ground once and the soil and grass flew a few meters away.

"Car!"

The hill was always deserted, but today of all days, there was a car parked at the top. There didn't seem to be anyone in the car. The smell was even stronger there, changing his hunch into a conviction. Keeping up his momentum, Ikuma jumped down from the hill.

"What? Nothing?"

When he landed there was no corpse there as he'd expected. There were bloodstains on the ground, as well as an incredibly intense smell, but he couldn't see a body anywhere.

"W-what's going on?"

In the darkness, it was hard to search the nearby area. *No way could another Ghoul have caught the scent and taken the corpse away,* he thought. Ikuma looked up at the sky, not knowing what to do. And that's when he realized someone was staring at him.

He screamed in shock and fell backward.

Ikuma's eyes popped wide open, his lips were bloodied, and

[THE BIG CITY]

he had twigs stuck to his body. Just like the prey of a butcherbird impaled on a branch for later, the man's corpse hung from a tree. He seemed to be in his fifties or thereabouts. *When I jumped down I never would've anticipated this*, Ikuma thought.

"H-how did you die?"

There was no reply to Ikuma's question, of course. Putting his hands on his hips, Ikuma pushed himself up and took a look at the man.

"Why did you have to die, hm?"

Ikuma gently brought his hands together and silently prayed for the man. Then, kicking at the soil and jumping up, he climbed the tree.

"This might hurt a little, sorry."

Ikuma put his weight on the branch of the tree that the man was stuck on, bending it until it snapped, and the man fell to the ground. Then he jumped down and pulled the branch from his body, which was lying on the grass. His eyes were fully open, as was his mouth, which looked like it was ready to scream. Ikuma wanted to close them both, but he realized it would probably be considered strange to go that far.

Ikuma looked the corpse over again. The man's right arm had extensive damage to it and looked like it might tear off even now.

"I'm really sorry . . ."

Ikuma put his hands together again before pulling the man's right arm off. *If I just leave it at this maybe they'll think a wild animal got at him.*

He put the arm in a plastic bag, wrapped it in a cloth, and slipped it into his bag. Ikuma put his hands together in prayer again over the man's body before leaving the scene.

"Better deal with this quickly."

When he got back home, Ikuma put the arm on a cutting board and got out a knife. He cut the meat off the bone, minced it, and formed it into meatballs. Then he put the meatballs in hot water along with the bone, waited for the water to come to a boil, and then removed them from the pan.

"Smells great," he said to himself.

But he wasn't going to eat it all now. He chilled the meatballs, wrapped them up, and put them all in the freezer.

He put the bone on the table, as well as a single cup of the broth.

"Thank you for this meal," he said, putting his hands together in gratitude, before drinking the broth.

"Yum . . ."

Next he gnawed at the pieces of meat that were stuck to the bone. Once he'd crunched away at it and gnawed it clean, his stomach was full. He reflected on how glad he was to have a small appetite.

Then he washed and dried the bone again before breaking it up with a hammer and turning it into bone meal.

This'll keep for a while, he thought.

Ikuma was filled with relief, but at the same time he also felt a sense of the meaninglessness of life well up inside him.

"I wish someone had been there for you, other than me," he muttered to himself, staring at the fridge. *But I eat people's tragedies.*

[THE BIG CITY]

"I'm no better than a hyena . . ."

He spent his days at his part-time job, and his nights looking for corpses. Any spare time he spent busking in front of train stations or in parks. What he really wanted was an audition in some big industry office somewhere, but he wasn't familiar with Tokyo yet so he didn't know what to do or where to go.

He was getting used to this area little by little, though. There seemed to be a lot of coffee shops around, because whenever he walked down the street he caught the smell of good coffee. He still couldn't afford that kind of indulgence, but one day, when he was on his feet, he wanted to try a cup of coffee at one of those places.

But he had one concern—wouldn't any good coffee shop be full of "his kind"?

"Oh, again?"

He'd finished work and was heading home on his bike when he caught the scent of his own kind. Every time he passed by this café called Anteiku he smelled Ghouls. Maybe this was their favorite hangout.

A shiver ran through Ikuma, and he started pedaling away as hard as he could.

"Don't wanna get too close . . ."

II

His life in Tokyo was going pretty well, all things considered. He got along well with people at work, and he could get food regularly. But that was only because lots of people killed themselves.

One day he was on his bike, heading toward the hill again. As he got closer to his feeding ground, the smell of death was in the air.

"Another dead one, huh . . ."

He was glad to get something to eat, but it also made him feel down. At the top of the hill Ikuma got off his bike and went down the slope by foot.

There, he found a young woman's body on the ground.

"Why do they want to die? Why did she . . ." he murmured, standing before the woman's bloody corpse. *If I'd met her just before she did this I would've tried to stop her.* In truth, he had stopped people from killing themselves more times than he could count.

But he couldn't let himself get too sentimental. He had a job to do, and it had to be done quickly. Ikuma reached out to touch her.

"So you're the one who's been causing all the mayhem around here lately."

Suddenly, someone's voice cut into the silence between Ikuma and the corpse. He turned around in surprise to see a man, his face cloaked by a hood. He looked to be in his late twenties to early thirties. He had a goatee and long hair that fell around his face.

He's a Ghoul.

0 0 4 [THE BIG CITY]

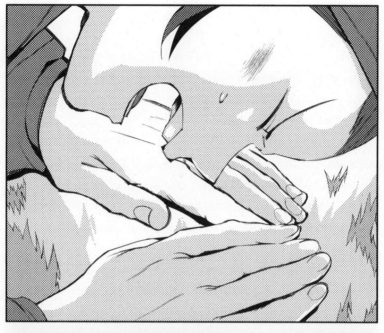

It was easy to see why Ikuma hadn't noticed him lurking there. He was a far, far more experienced Ghoul.

Ikuma left the corpse where she was and dashed back up the slope. *I gotta get away from here somehow.* But right when he reached the top, a shadow entered his field of view.

He yelped in shock.

The man had already made it to the top of the hill, confronting him there like an ambusher. Immediately, the man's fist met Ikuma's face with a force that sent him tumbling back down the slope.

Reflexively he tumbled as he fell, but as his body hit the ground he felt dizzy. The man approached silently. His breathing didn't even seem to have changed.

I can't beat him. I know that already.

"I'm so sorry!"

Ikuma rolled over into a bow, his hands on the ground and his head lowered.

"I just moved to Tokyo and I don't know how things work here! I didn't know this was somebody's turf! I'm sorry, I won't come here again! Please overlook this, I'm begging you!"

The man was silent for a second. "You don't know how things work? When did you move here?"

"About three months ago," Ikuma stuttered.

"Three months? And in all that time, you had zero contact with other Ghouls?"

Ikuma warily raised his head and nodded.

"You're the first I've met since I moved here. You might not understand, but I want to live in the human world—well, as much as I can. So I've been trying to avoid other Ghouls . . ."

His words were unexpected to the man, who looked like he was deep in thought. Like a criminal awaiting sentencing, Ikuma waited for his response.

He looked straight at Ikuma. "Oh," he muttered. "You're like Ken."

"Ken?"

Who's this Ken? The man didn't answer Ikuma, but he took a piece of paper that looked like a flier out of his coat pocket and handed it to him. On the paper was the name of a café, Anteiku, and its address.

"This is . . ."

. . . the café that always reeks of Ghouls.

"The people here are in charge of dividing up the 20th Ward. It's used as an information exchange for Ghouls too. It'd be useful for you if you dropped in once." He paused. "I'll let you off this time." With that, the man left.

Ikuma looked at the flier and at the woman's body, and for a while he couldn't make himself leave the spot, but eventually he ran away, leaving the area without laying another hand on the corpse.

III

A few weeks went by after his encounter with the mysterious man before Ikuma got hungry. He took the spice jar that he'd put the bone meal in to save for hard times and nearly put it in his mouth as he shook it, but nothing came out. It was still a while until payday, so he couldn't even buy himself coffee.

I'm not going to Anteiku no matter what. I don't want anything to do with other Ghouls, it's too scary. I'll deal with this somehow.

But now that he knew the Ghouls here had their own territories, he couldn't go looking for bodies in the same happy-go-lucky way he used to.

"I'm so screwed . . . Is everyone in Tokyo like that guy?"

Since he'd seen a glimpse of that man's powers, Ikuma's fear of Ghouls in Tokyo had only grown. His stomach growled. *I could starve like this.*

"Mama . . ."

If I ask mom she'll send me some meat and money. Then I could keep going. Without really thinking about it Ikuma grabbed his smartphone. His hands were shaking as he fumbled with the screen.

But then he almost flung it across the room. *Why did I come to Tokyo in the first place? To make it on my own. So why the hell would I press the emergency button and call mom now?*

Sitting at home, all he could think about was his hunger. Ikuma put his guitar on his back and went out.

 # 0 0 4 [THE BIG CITY]

It was six in the evening. He sat down in front of the station, awash with people coming home from work, and started playing one of his own songs. It was a folky song, the kind of music his mother liked to listen to.

Ikuma had a reason for what he sang. *I want to lose myself in the crowd, be like any other person, but I'm a monster. My life depends on eating people's sadness. And I sometimes feel fate's gotten the best of me. I'm being crushed by the contradictions . . .* He put his feelings into his lyrics, and singing helped him keep a kind of emotional equilibrium.

Keep going, you can do it, don't give up, you've still got life.

It was his hope that this song might give encouragement to someone. *I want to think, want to believe that even a Ghoul like me can give support to humans. I want to be a cog in the machine of the world.*

As he sang his voice started sounding better. His high spirits were overriding the feeling of hunger. Suddenly, he had an audience of one.

The boy watching him was about the same age, or perhaps a little younger, with short, ruffled brown hair. He sat down right in front of Ikuma and listened to his song.

Ikuma found it so much easier to sing to an audience. He started playing a song he had written since moving to Tokyo.

"God is there, yeah, don't lose sight . . ." he sang.

It was something he thought when he looked at all the people who had cut their own lives short, and he wondered if maybe there was something that had made them cut all ties to everyone and everything. He wondered if the truth wasn't that there was something really important, very near.

He knew it was absurd for him to be thinking that kind of thing, when he was the one who ate their flesh. But he couldn't help it. When he closed his eyes and listened carefully, he felt a presence that he knew would save him—God.

"God?"

The boy, who had been silently listening, suddenly responded. The way he said it, it sounded like he wished God were there. *Maybe he's in the kind of situation that makes you seek God's help.*

Once he finished singing, Ikuma took his hands away from the strings and spoke to the boy.

"Is something troubling you?"

For a second he gave no response. Then he startled, suddenly aware, and rushed to applaud. But his gaze quickly fell.

After a moment of silence it all started to spill out.

"It's just . . . my friend's in trouble and I want to help him but I can't in any big way." Ikuma didn't know what had happened, but it seemed like the boy was lamenting his own powerlessness. "If there is a God, I need their help," he continued. His words sounded strangely sad.

Trouble with his friend . . .

Ikuma remembered his friends back home.

"But you know, it's okay, isn't it? You don't have to do anything big to help."

 # 0 0 4 [THE BIG CITY]

Ikuma had lots of friends. Human friends, and a few Ghoul friends too. But since moving to Tokyo, he still hadn't met a single person that he could call a friend.

He couldn't bear the thought of life without friends by his side to laugh and fight with over silly stuff. His life alone was a sad one, and sometimes he cried a little at night. Now he knew it was enough just to have a friend by your side.

"Sometimes it helps just to be someone's friend. I think there's nothing better than that," he told the boy, choosing his words carefully.

As Ikuma wondered whether he had gotten too preachy, the boy nodded, as if he'd been chewing over the words.

"I'm feeling a little better already!" he said, with a smile like the sun breaking through clouds. When he smiled he looked younger.

I think this is the first time I've been of any use to someone since I moved here.

The boy offered him some money in gratitude, but Ikuma refused it. It had been like a ray of light cutting through the gloom of his life in Tokyo, and now Ikuma himself finally felt positive. That was reward enough for him.

But the boy couldn't let it go at that. He rummaged in his backpack, looking for something to give Ikuma.

"Oh, I should give you something to say thank you."

He fumbled for his jacket pocket as if he'd suddenly remembered something. And what he pulled out brought a smile to Ikuma's face.

It was a can of coffee. And best of all, it was unsweetened with no milk.

I can't get food, I'm out of money, and I'm starving, but there is no gift in the world more precious than this.

"This helps a lot. God's work!"

Ikuma grinned as he held the can in both his hands reverently, as if he were praying.

"I'll come back and listen again. And I'll bring my friend next time!" the boy said, then left.

He sure is a lucky guy to have a friend who worries about him that much.

"Whoa."

While he was talking to the boy, a crowd had gathered around without him noticing. Ikuma picked up his guitar and again began to sing.

He sang in front of the station for a few hours. Prompted by the boy's presence, his audience had grown, and lots of people had listened to his songs. Some of them had been generous, and he managed to make nearly 6,000 yen. Now he could buy all the coffee he wanted to stifle his hunger.

He'd imagined Tokyo as a scary place, but now he knew there were some very kind people there, too. *I'm gonna find a way to get my own food somehow and make it in Tokyo.*

As he walked down a road with no one else on it, going away from the station, he opened the can of coffee the boy had given him. The aroma that drifted up toward him delighted his sense of smell. Just one whiff was enough to know how it tasted.

Ikuma slowly brought the can up to his mouth.

[THE BIG CITY]

"Just my luck to run into a Ghoul in a place like this! I've been blessed, no exaggeration!"

The voice came out of nowhere.

Ikuma exclaimed in surprise.

Before he could even turn around, he was punched in the hand holding the can of coffee. Then, not knowing what had happened to him, Ikuma felt an intense pain shooting through his thigh and fell straight to the ground.

"Wh . . ."

A small puddle formed around the can of coffee where it fell, and his guitar also lay nearby. As the pain spread through him, he realized belatedly that someone had kicked him.

"Any self-respecting Ghoul shouldn't drink that cheap canned coffee. You've gotta go for the artisan, pour-over stuff."

Sensing danger to his body, Ikuma tried to get up and run away, but this time, a fist connected with his jaw.

He was sent flying, and landed on the ground again.

"W-why?"

That's when, finally, Ikuma took a good look at his assailant. He had the looks of a movie star or a model. At first glance, he didn't look like a violent kind of guy at all.

But his red eyes and the gleeful smile on his lips told Ikuma all he needed to know. *This guy is extremely dangerous.*

"Listen up! The thing is, tomorrow I'm having a long-awaited feast, after months and years of pushing myself to extremes! Can you hear how my heart is pounding? I hope you can!"

To Ikuma this was a meaningless string of words.

Maybe he didn't want to be understood either. *Maybe just taking out that passion on someone is enough for him.*

His heel slammed into Ikuma's solar plexus.

Ikuma screamed in pain.

A number of his ribs cracked with a dull crunching sound.

"I know you can feel it, this pathos overflowing from me! But humans are too fragile to share this feeling . . . Anyone but a Ghoul would break too easily!"

He was not like the man who had given Ikuma the flier for Anteiku. His punches were meant to kill.

"Oh, I'm sorry, I didn't introduce myself," the man said, looking down at Ikuma. "My name is Shu Tsukiyama, although there's no need for you to remember that!"

Ikuma's body twisted as Tsukiyama kicked him. His right foot sped through the air, aimed directly at Ikuma's heart.

"Uh-oh."

There was the sound of a blunt impact, like something hitting metal. Whatever it was had impeded the movement of Tsukiyama's heel.

Blood was pouring from Ikuma's mouth all over his face, but near his left arm a thick Kokaku kagune, shaped like a turtle's shell, had emerged. Reminiscent of a knight's shield, it somehow repelled Tsukiyama's blows.

"Oh, you're a Kokaku, too, huh?" Tsukiyama said with a jeering smile after a long appraisal of Ikuma's kagune. "Then take a look at *my* kagune!"

[THE BIG CITY]

Something ominous rose up from Tsukiyama's back before swirling and twisting itself around Tsukiyama's arms.

"How do you like that!"

His kagune was shaped like a drill, and Ikuma could see just by looking how heavy it was. *How much upkeep does it take just to have a kagune like that*?

The cruel reality had been shoved in his face. They both had a Kokaku, and the one to win would be, quite simply, the one who was strongest.

"Take this!"

Tsukiyama's kagune came at Ikuma, aimed directly at his face. Ikuma jumped backward to get some distance, but Tsukiyama's

kagune was more flexible than its thickness suggested, and it also seemed to extend like a spring.

"Gaaaaaaaaaaaaaaaah!"

Instantly, he tried to protect himself with his own Kagune, but his could not withstand the weight of the blow, and it pierced his shoulder. The feeling of it twisting through his flesh made his screams even louder.

Ikuma's body rose up, then fell at once.

Death . . .

That's the only way I can see out of this.

But the relentless pain of slamming into concrete didn't hit Ikuma. Instead, he heard something break with a cracking sound. Ikuma guessed instantly what had broken his fall.

"My guitar!"

"Huh?"

Tsukiyama stopped attacking.

Ikuma got up and took a look at what had been crushed under him.

"Dammit, no way!"

He opened the guitar case. Inside he saw his beloved guitar, the one he'd brought all the way from home. Parts of the body and the neck were broken, and there was extensive damage. There was no way he could play it like this.

"No!"

Ikuma crouched over the guitar, cradling it in his arms.

"Is that your guitar, then?" Tsukiyama said, coming near.

0 0 4   [THE BIG CITY]

"Just leave me alone!" Ikuma cried.

Ikuma brought his kagune out again and rammed it straight at Tsukiyama.

"Calm down, give me time to assess the situation too!"

Tsukiyama slid away, avoiding the attack. Ikuma fell back to the ground, panting. His kagune disappeared; he was no longer in a fit state to fight.

"What have we here, Tsukiyama? Oh no, did you break somebody's guitar?"

Even as he heard the mysterious voice, Ikuma thought he must've been imagining it. This girl who'd wandered right into the site of a slaughter without any affectations could be nothing other than an illusion.

She peered into the guitar case. "Looks like it was well loved, too. What kind of songs do you play?" she said sympathetically. This got Tsukiyama's attention. He clapped his hands to his head and turned his eyes skyward.

"Jesus! I've . . . broken . . . this guy's guitar?!"

His kagune disappeared immediately.

"Thank you, Hori. You always open my eyes for me. You're the only one who stands by me with such tenderness."

"I'm not standing by you, though," said the girl he'd called Hori, completely rejecting what he'd said.

Tsukiyama did not take notice, laughing happily. "Oh, Hori, your jokes are so polished! You're hilarious. So unique!" But then he turned to Ikuma and lowered his eyebrows in an expression of penitence.

"I have done something unforgivable to you. How could I have known you were a music lover, just like me?"

He put his hand to his chest and bowed his head like a gentleman.

"And what I've done to your instrument is pathetic. I'm going to tell my friend at the music store what happened. Maybe we can work something out." He took a business card out of his wallet and stuck it in Ikuma's guitar case. "Give them my name when you go.

"You've been mortally wounded, but if you eat it might do something for you. I should go procure some food for you, properly speaking, but ironically, I'm busy preparing for tomorrow. When you're better I'd love to hear your songs. Now, I must beg your pardon."

With that, Tsukiyama and the girl disappeared into the darkness. Ikuma stood up, holding the wound on his shoulder.

"Oh man . . . This is bad . . ."

He had lost a ton of blood, his body had sustained massive injuries, and a ferocious hunger was welling up within him. His eyes gleamed a fiery red, and in this state he wouldn't be able to resist attacking a living person to kill and eat them.

But that's the one thing I won't do!

"What do I do . . ."

All logic disappeared from his mind, and as he racked his brain he finally came up with something.

"Ante . . . iku . . ."

How ironic is it that I've avoided Ghouls all this time, only to be attacked by a Ghoul, and my last resort means relying on Ghouls?

Ikuma put his guitar case on his back and headed for Anteiku.

An intense pain shot through him with every step, and as he walked his Ghoul instincts coursed through his body. Reason and instinct became entwined in his mind, and he felt like he was losing his mind.

"God is . . . there . . ."

Ikuma began singing his own song, his voice thick and hoarse. His voice barely made a sound, and it kept breaking, but he sang with all his might.

"Don't . . . lose sight . . ."

Ikuma turned the corner and finally saw the café ahead of him. It was late, but luckily the lights were still on.

They'll help me somehow, he thought.

Just then, he collapsed on the spot, the relief perhaps having taken the energy right out of him. And he lay there, unable to move.

"No . . . way . . ."

Ikuma put both of his hands against the ground and tried to push himself up somehow. But his elbow was broken, and his energy left him. It wasn't memories or regrets that ran through his mind as he faced death.

I want . . . I want . . . I want to eat someone!

It was a greedy cry for food.

"Wh . . . why?"

Ikuma balled his hands up into fists and groaned mournfully.

"Why? Why do we . . ."

Hot tears ran down his cheeks.

"Why do we have to eat humans?"

All of his energy had been used up now. He couldn't take one step.

"Hey there, are you okay?"

Oh God, I've been found by a woman on her way home from the office.

And she smells delicious.

She approached him cautiously.

Ikuma's heart leapt. As his pulse pounded, blood coursed through his body. Ghoul blood.

Do it, man, eat her. You're hungry, right? What are you waiting for?

His instinct, now surpassing his reason, called to him. He could not fight the Ghoul blood he was drenched in.

Oh, this is it. This is why they want to take their own lives, he thought to himself, probably in the same instant.

"Hey, what happened?"

Suddenly, he heard loud banging noises nearby. The woman stood up, surprised, and looked in the direction they'd been heard from.

"It's rockets . . . fireworks?"

The sound brought Ikuma back to his senses. He felt the heaviness of the guitar on his back, and he gritted his teeth.

Then, in the direction of the noise, he saw something enormously frightening. It sent chills down his spine so cold that it was hard to breathe. Something Ghouls must avoid at any cost was there.

"What's all this commotion?"

0 0 4   [THE BIG CITY]

Just then, a girl with black hair came dashing out of Anteiku. She looked in the same direction as Ikuma before turning her attention to him in surprise.

"Touka, do you know what just . . ."

Next, a boy with dark hair appeared from inside the shop. His eyes followed the girl's over to Ikuma in astonishment. Ikuma could see his own bright-red eyes reflected clearly in the boy's eyes.

"Are you all right?"

He rushed over to Ikuma and covered his red eyes with his own hand to hide them.

I'm saved.

Ikuma closed his eyes before letting go of consciousness.

IV

The smell of coffee hit him.

It was that smell that reeled him in and made him open his eyes. Slowly the ceiling came into view.

"Has he come to?" he heard someone near him say. The room was tinged by soft sunlight.

"I . . ."

With his head in his hands he tried to sit up, but the boy who seemed to be taking care of him said, "You should try to sleep a little longer," and forced him to lie back down.

"You're at a café called Anteiku. My name is Ken Kaneki."

"Ken . . ."

That's the name the guy told me when I had a run-in with him at the suicide spot. Was he talking about this boy?

"How are your injuries?"

Ikuma closed his hands into fists and let them go again. He could move his hands perfectly fine. That ferocious hunger had already disappeared, and both his body and mind felt calmer.

I've been saved, Ikuma again realized. But he was horrified at the same time.

I had no idea starvation would be so intense.

If it hadn't have been for those fireworks and these guys showing up, I would've killed and eaten that kind woman who asked if I was okay.

"Yomo told me a little about you. He said you've been trying to avoid other Ghouls and blend in with human society."

Is that the guy from the suicide hot spot?

Ikuma took another look at the boy who'd introduced himself as Kaneki. He had a distinctive smell to him, a mix of the smell of a female Ghoul and a human.

Kaneki looked at Ikuma, who was silent. "Oh, sorry! It's all right if you don't want to talk. You must be very tired still . . ." he apologized as if he had been out of line.

He was not so much curious as he had a desire to understand things deeply, by experiencing them directly. He was a kind of Ghoul that Ikuma had rarely seen before. *I think he's a little bit like me.*

"My mother... was a human," Ikuma said, laying it right out there, as if he had been invited to by the uniqueness of the situation.

"What?" Kaneki said, confused. "What do you mean? Do you mean that you... used to be a human too?"

He could sense Kaneki's unease as he said the word "too" but Ikuma shook his head.

"I've been a Ghoul since the day I was born. But I was raised by humans."

Ikuma began to tell Kaneki a little of his story.

My mother is a top surgeon. And her husband was a doctor too.

But they found it difficult to conceive a child together, and finally, after undergoing fertility treatments, they had a child after seven years of marriage.

They were delighted, and they took their roles as parents seriously.

But six months after the birth, her husband collapsed from over-working and died.

My mother was grief-stricken. She could not forgive herself for not noticing her husband's grave state even though she was a doctor.

But my mother still had a child to take care of.

She knew she had to be both mother and father, and do it well. That thought was enough to make her go on living.

But a few days before the child's first birthday, it happened.

The child died.

The child always got cranky at night, but that night and that night only, he fell fast asleep.

My mother woke up in the middle of the night. "Sound asleep, aren't you?" But when she caressed the child's cheek, he was incredibly cold.

My mother frantically tried to resuscitate him. The child did not come back to life.

She had now lost everything. The only thing she had left to lose was her sanity. She wandered through the town in the pouring rain, clutching her dead child in her arms.

Let me die too, she thought. But as she wandered, she saw a woman lying down, hiding in the shadow of a building.

Perhaps it was her instincts as a doctor that made her do what she did next.

Just as she asked the woman if she was all right, the woman looked at her.

With pure red eyes.

My mother went weak in the knees at this grotesque sight, and she was paralyzed with fear. But just then she heard a baby begin to wail.

She stared at the woman unthinkingly. The woman had a baby no more than a year old clutched to her chest.

My mother saw that the woman had wounds all over her, but there was not a scratch on the child.

She had been defending the child from harm.

Now it was the woman's turn to look at the child cradled against my mother's chest. The woman's eyes grew wider with surprise.

My mother turned away in a hurry to hide, but the woman apparently had noticed that the baby was dead.

 # 0 0 4 [THE BIG CITY]

"Please . . ."

The woman held out the child with trembling hands toward my mother.

"Save this child . . ."

My mother heard men shouting in the distance.

"She must've run this way!"

"I'm gonna find you!"

My mother understood then. That the woman was a Ghoul, and that the child was as well.

The baby started crying weakly.

"I hear the baby!"

At the same time, my mother understood something else.

That the woman was also a mother, the same as her. And that the woman loved this child just as much as she loved her own child.

My mother took the Ghoul child in her arms and handed her own child to the woman.

"Thank you . . ."

My mother ran off. As she did, the Ghoul woman whispered, "I'm so sorry, just a little bit . . ." and started nibbling on my mother's child.

Having eaten a little flesh, the woman was able to push herself to the limits of her strength. She stood up and went running in the opposite direction from my mother.

"She was just here!"

Aware that there were multiple men chasing after the woman, my mother ran through the rain like a woman possessed.

The next morning in the newspaper she saw a story about a Ghoul mother and child.

A Ghoul mother, cornered by investigators, had apparently jumped into the sea, still clutching a child. The mother's body had been found but the child's had not.

My mother read the article with the child in her arms. That child was me.

It was a secret too large to deal with on her own. She confided in her parents. When she told them, they nearly fainted from shock, but eventually they accepted it after seeing how determined my mother was.

My mother returned to work at the hospital early. During the day, she dropped me off with my grandparents, and in the evening she would give me "food" she had procured from the hospital.

She taught me from a relatively early age that I was a Ghoul. And she was very open with me about what kind of standing Ghouls have in the human world.

And she raised me as a human.

When I was a small child and unable to control my feelings I stayed at home, but when I got older I went to primary school, like any other child my age. My mother told the school that I had food allergies, and she always packed a lunch for me.

So I was raised with human values. Of course I've never killed anyone.

"I think my mother wishes I would've become a doctor, but I don't have the head for it. Plus I have my own dreams," Ikuma said. His broken guitar sat next to his cot.

"They say songs can cross borders. It doesn't matter if you're a Ghoul or if you're human. I just think, like, it would be great if I could write a song that really reached people. But maybe it's stupid for a kid from the country to have that dream . . ."

"Of course it isn't!" Kaneki said immediately, rejecting Ikuma's self-deprecation. He paused. "It makes me happy to hear that a Ghoul like you feels so close to humans." Kaneki spoke as if he were representing all humans. "I've got your back."

Ikuma didn't know what to make of this mysterious boy who smelled like both a human and a Ghoul. But for some reason, what he'd said had made Ikuma feel like he could realize his crazy dream.

A few weeks after he was rescued by the people at Anteiku, Ikuma was busking in front of the station. The guitar in his arms was the well-loved one he'd brought all the way from home.

After what happened, Ikuma had actually gone to the music store that Tsukiyama had recommended. He had been afraid, but he'd also felt that he had a legitimate right to compensation from the person who broke his guitar.

The owner of the store had heard about what happened from Tsukiyama, and he offered to provide Ikuma with any used guitar, free of charge.

But Ikuma told him that he wanted his own guitar fixed. No guitar but the one he'd brought from his hometown would do.

The strings had snapped, the body and neck had broken and split into two pieces, and everywhere he looked he could see damage. It looked like it would be impossible to repair.

But the owner said, without hesitation, "Well, Tsukiyama said to do what I could," and Ikuma had no idea how he'd done it, but a few days later the owner returned the guitar to him, restored.

As for the problem of how to obtain food that had been plaguing him, through an arrangement made by the manager at Anteiku, the famous suicide spot where he had originally been getting food was handed over to him as his "territory."

They had also told him that Anteiku could provide him with

meat they had procured, but he thought he would forget the gravity of a life if he got used to just being given meat.

By facing people's deaths and getting his own food by himself, he could not forget that he was a Ghoul, which was something he thought was important in order for him to continue living in human society.

Fortunately, his territory was in the middle of nowhere, so there were no other Ghouls around there, either.

During a small break in songs, something took him by surprise. He was taking a drink from a can of coffee when a boy ran over waving, saying, "Hello-o!

"Remember me? I heard you here before. My name's Hideyoshi Nagachika! But everyone calls me Hide!"

"Of course I remember you, man. Okay, Hide it is. I'll be sure to call you that from now on."

Hide smiled broadly at hearing Ikuma say his name.

"Oh, and I brought my friend, too! Kaneki—hey, Kaneki!" Hide yelled, turning around.

Kaneki?

He looked in surprise to see another boy come rushing up.

"Man, Hide, I said you were too excited."

He had black hair and wore an eye patch over his left eye. And he had the smell of a human mixed with a Ghoul.

When he realized Ikuma was standing there, his eye popped in surprise.

"Uh, so, Hide, who's this artist you've been talking about?"

"This guy! Sorry, can I, uh, ask your name?"

Ikuma thought about the pain that Hide had showed him after listening to his song. And he thought about the unique smell that Kaneki had, making it hard to tell which side he was on.

"Did you used to be a human, too?"

What Kaneki had said at Anteiku came back to Ikuma. He felt that he'd seen a glimpse of their anguish and its cause. But Ikuma introduced himself, sounding cheerful.

"I'm Ikuma Momochi. And you are . . . ?" he asked Kaneki, pretending it was the first time they'd met. Kaneki stood up straight and introduced himself.

"I'm Kaneki, Ken Kaneki," he said.

Ikuma began plucking at the guitar strings.

"Well, since you guys came all this way, you might as well listen to a song!"

This town is so much more terrifying than I imagined, and so much kinder, too.

He started singing a song he'd written since moving to Tokyo.

Ikuma Momochi, a Ghoul living in Tokyo.

 # 0 0 4 [THE BIG CITY]

[**THE BOOKMARK**]

ow can I reach out to the world I'm aiming for?

"Who were those 'suspicious characters' after all?" Kaneki said to Touka, who was cleaning up in the café as Kaneki dried the freshly washed coffee cups.

She picked up another piece of trash. "Probably investigators," she said blankly.

It was a few weeks after Yoshimoto had told them to be careful because suspicious characters had been spotted in the area.

Kaneki had told his friend Hide not to come around the café, and the staff themselves had felt on edge and tense on a daily basis since then, but that day their manager had reported to them that nobody had been spotted for a while.

As Touka said, it hadn't been that long since a Ghoul was killed by investigators close to the café. He wasn't a Ghoul from the 20th Ward, but he had come in for a coffee once.

On one hand, he'd also heard about a Ghoul named Ikuma who had moved to Tokyo from the countryside and had passed by the café a few times. Ikuma apparently wanted nothing to do with other Ghouls, and he acted in secret, so it wasn't impossible that Yoshimura had picked up on him and decided he was suspicious.

And it wasn't just that. He'd also heard rumors about a gawky college-age boy with glasses hanging around the area. Kaneki didn't know which was the true story.

What was for certain, though, was that there definitely had been suspicious people around, that something had happened, and that Yoshimura had made a judgment call.

"Maybe things will be a little quieter now . . ."

"There's no such thing as quiet in the Ghoul world."

He'd mainly been talking to himself, but Touka shot him down anyway. *She's probably right. There's no rest for Ghouls.*

"But always being on alert wears you out."

Being able to breathe was important for more than just staying alive. But Touka just dismissed him as a "wuss." She wasn't going to throw him a life preserver.

But he was kind of used to her now. She treated everyone else who worked at Anteiku the same way, as well as some of the regulars. And Kaneki thought that he'd grown a lot since the days when he rejected everything about being a Ghoul.

Despite all that, there was someone who weighed heavily on

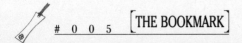

0 0 5　[THE BOOKMARK]

Kaneki's mind lately. He was worried about Hinami Fueguchi, the girl who had lost both of her parents and was currently living with Touka. She was sometimes shy, but she was a kind, sweet girl. He worried that she was sad.

She was living with Touka, but Touka had to go to school, and she often got home late after her shifts at Anteiku. Sometimes Hinami came to the café, and Kaneki talked to her or taught her kanji, but it wasn't enough.

Hinami spent the majority of her time alone in Touka's house. Kaneki wondered if she spent her time alone dwelling on things: her beloved parents, the terrifying investigators, all the conflicts in her own life as a Ghoul.

Especially seeing her mother killed in front of her own eyes. She had always been there for Hinami, protecting her. It was like she was missing an important part of herself. There was no way she could not be in some kind of pain. When Kaneki thought about it, it made his own chest ache.

"Hey, Touka. How's Hinami doing these days?"

"Oh, fine as usual."

But his only source of information only gave him a halfhearted answer. He wanted to hear more about her, but Touka just stared at him and said, "Give me a hand so we can get this over with." The conversation seemed like it was over; she was in an even worse mood now. He could see an aura of anger over her. *She'll kill me if I say one more word.* He started putting the clean dishes away as a way to avoid her. She was still glaring at him.

The author Saneatsu Mushanokouji put it like this in *On Life*: "To feel the fear of death, one must still have work to do while they are alive."

I want to be a bridge, telling Ghouls how people feel and letting people know what Ghouls think and feel. Because there's nothing but hatred between the two groups now, but if each had an understanding of the other, I think that could change. Even if my presence is unwanted, I still want to be involved with both humans and Ghouls.

And he felt the same about Hinami. While Touka's attitude seemed to say, "Don't get involved," Kaneki himself had the right to worry about her, and if he had his way he'd like to help her move forward in a better direction.

"Hm, what should I do?"

Sitting in the auditorium at the end of a class at his college, Kaneki wondered to himself what he could do to make Hinami happier.

"She needs a hobby . . ."

Maybe he was being too simplistic, but he got the feeling that she wouldn't be so sad about being alone all the time if she had something she could devote herself to. But Kaneki himself had a very small repertoire of things he did at home alone, and the only thing that came to mind was reading.

He headed off to Anteiku for his shift, backpack on his shoulders, with his arms folded.

"But she does like books by Takatsugi, so maybe reading's not such a bad idea."

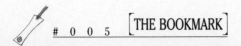 # 0 0 5 [THE BOOKMARK]

Hinami loved to read books by Sen Takatsugi, who was also Kaneki's favorite author. Books were, on one level, a means of absorbing knowledge, so why wouldn't it be good for Hinami to read other books, not just ones by Takatsugi?

He was thinking about buying kids' books for her from used bookstores or the Internet when he suddenly thought about what it must be like to have Touka as a landlord.

"Books take up a lot of space. Touka would hate that . . ."

The thing about books was, the more you read and liked them, the more you wanted to have on hand to read. Before you knew it you needed more bookshelves, and then all of a sudden they filled your house.

But Touka's house was a reflection of her own personality: simple, with not much in it. If books started taking up too much room, she might get angry. And not just at Hinami, but at Kaneki too.

So he went back to square one. Kaneki looked around him, hoping he'd hit on a good idea.

"Aha!"

He had it. And the timing couldn't have been better.

Right in front of him Kaneki saw the library.

"Hey, Touka, the next time you've got a minute, why not take Hinami to the library?"

As soon as he got to Anteiku he ran up to Touka and made his suggestion, but she gave him a confused and doubtful look. Not about to let her negative reaction get him down, Kaneki continued.

"I know Hinami spends nearly all her time in the house. She

must get bored when she's alone. So she could check out books she likes from the library . . ."

"The investigators know about her. And they got a guy not long ago near the café. So, no," Touka said.

There was no way she could go outside without taking extreme precautions. Touka's opinion was also out of concern for Hinami.

"If you just pay close attention, then . . . Look, if she's in the house all the time it's not good for more than just her mental health."

"Anyone can pay close attention. Like, you could," she said.

"I, uh . . ."

"But if something happened, it'd be your responsibility. The suspicious characters hanging around the café might be gone, but this area's still full of danger, you know."

He had thought it might go like this, but Touka made her disapproval very apparent. He could see that what she said was right in parts, but he couldn't come up with a rebuttal.

"But she must have all kinds of things running through her mind, sitting at home alone."

So Kaneki tried a purely emotional argument.

"Thoughts about her mother, or about her father . . . Even if she wants to move on, it must be hard when she remembers what happened, and she must be sad. Those kind of feelings can eat away at you."

Even Touka had nothing to say to that.

"But she's trying hard not to show it to us. I think she's just keeping it all to herself so she doesn't make anybody worried," Kaneki said, adding that it was because she was a sweet kid.

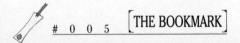# 0 0 5 [THE BOOKMARK]

"Fiction books give the reader a chance to step away from their own reality and into the shoes of the characters, and they show you a world that isn't the one you already know. And sometimes the story's not so different from your own, and it lets you get closer to your own feelings," he said.

Sometimes you're confronted with the ugly parts of yourself that you don't want to see, but books can also tell you a lot about the things you don't notice when you're just trying to get through somehow.

"So when you close a book you've just finished reading and return to reality, all the pain and sadness you couldn't put into words before are still there on those pages. And that can be comforting. So I think reading could do a lot to help Hinami."

I've said all I wanted to say. All I can do now is wait for Touka's answer.

"What are you saying, you weirdo?"

"What?"

Touka was slightly weirded out. It seemed like Kaneki's argument did not resonate with her at all.

"But, but—seriously! Hinami loves to read, so I think it would be a nice change of pace for her."

Kaneki was getting discouraged. Touka folded her arms and sighed in resignation.

"Sunday, 2:00 p.m. In front of the library."

"What?"

Kaneki had heard her but didn't understand. Touka put her hands on her hips.

"What you were just talking about! The library!" she yelled. "Anyway, I don't know anything about books," she grumbled and turned away. *I guess she agrees.*

"Thanks," he stuttered.

"This is all about Hinami. No need to thank me."

"But . . ."

"Shut up!"

II

On Sunday, Kaneki got there five minutes before they were supposed to meet. He was standing in front of the library reading a paperback while he waited for Touka, who he thought would probably be late, when she appeared.

"Wait, why are you here so early?" he asked, putting his book back in his bag.

"Hinami," she said, turning around.

"Thank you, Mr. Kaneki!"

Although her face was hidden underneath a hat that was pulled down, Hinami's smile reached her entire face.

"She's been worried since yesterday, because she thought if we were late she might not be allowed to get books," Touka said, giving Kaneki a mean look.

Kaneki laughed drily. "Well, shall we?" he said to Hinami,

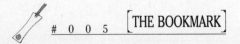

0 0 5 ⌈THE BOOKMARK⌋

before darting into the library like he was running away from something.

"Wow..."

She was amazed by the rows and rows of bookshelves holding countless books. With her hat off because it actually made her stand out more inside the library, Hinami's eyes danced with excitement at the crowded shelves of books.

"Mr. Kaneki, can I look at everything?"

"Of course you can. As long as you've got a library card, you can check out whatever you like. Pick a book," he told her. She timidly reached out to the shelves. She took one book out and flipped through the pages before taking out the one next to it and checking it, too.

"Wow, they've all got so many words," she said.

It took very little to impress her. Seeing her that happy was enough to prove it was worth taking her. But there were far too many books and she didn't seem to know how to choose one.

"They have some books by Takatsugi, but how about a children's book instead?"

Kaneki picked out a few books that he had read as a child and gave them to Hinami.

"Mr. Kaneki, is it okay if I read for a little while?"

"How about it, Touka?"

She hesitated. "Just for a minute or two."

Hinami sat down in one of the chairs in the reading room and started reading one of the books Kaneki had picked for her. He and Touka sat down beside her.

"Look, Mr. Kaneki. This book tells you how to say the words."

Unlike the books by Sen Takatsugi she was always reading, the children's books gave pronunciations for kanji. The content must have been much clearer and easier for her to read too. Since all of Hinami's learning came from books, this was perhaps a better way to build basic academic skills.

And of course, if her reading comprehension improved, she'd enjoy Sen Takatsugi's books even more.

But since Takatsugi's novels were Hinami's standard for books, her vocabulary was a little warped.

"This word isn't used like this in the books I always read," she said.

"Oh, that's because Takatsugi uses words in unique ways. In general it's used like this," he told her.

"Do words mean the same thing when they're written in hiragana as they mean in kanji?"

"It just makes it easier to read if a word is written in hiragana, that's all. The meaning is the same."

"Wait, is this Tsukumogami's island?" she asked.

"Oh. That says Kuju-ku islands. It's written with the same characters as Tsukumogami, the old lady with the white hair that shows up sometimes in Takatsugi's books."

Hinami was struggling more than he'd expected. Kaneki dealt with each of her questions patiently and thoroughly.

"Okey-dokey."

Just then, an eight- or nine-year-old boy with a book under his arm came and sat down near Hinami.

He started reading the book he'd brought with him, but something drew his attention to Hinami, who was asking about the most minute details about words. He glanced over at the book she was reading, then tilted his head.

"What's wrong with you, can't you read?" he asked.

He was confused at the sight of a girl older than himself who couldn't even read a kids' book.

Hinami looked at him in surprise. The color drained from Kaneki's and Touka's faces. They hadn't imagined that someone she'd never seen or met before would say that kind of thing to her.

The boy seemed to realize that he'd said something he shouldn't have and clapped his hand over his mouth.

"You little bastard," Touka muttered.

"Touka!"

Filled with anger, Touka stood up and started to make a move toward the boy.

"I, I'm sorry, kid, but get out of here, right now!" Kaneki yelled, pushing Touka away from him. She still looked ready to hit the boy. He was so scared by Touka's hostility that he couldn't speak, and he ran away with his book.

"Yeah, you better run!"

"Calm down, Touka."

She thinks if someone attacks you, you've gotta hit back. Touka watched the boy run off.

"Is it really that weird that I can't read?" Hinami had been frozen since the boy had talked to her.

"Hinami, it's..."

It wasn't that uncommon for Ghouls not to be able to read or write. But it was a different story for humans. A human child Hinami's age should have been able to read a book at that level easily.

Ghoul or human? Kaneki didn't know which side of the divide he should stand on in order to comfort her.

"Not at all, so don't worry too much about what kids like that say to you," Touka said, jumping in. Kaneki nodded in agreement with everything she said.

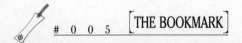
0 0 5 [THE BOOKMARK]

But Hinami closed the book she had been reading, and her shoulders slumped.

In the end, with Hinami feeling so down, Kaneki chose a few books for her before they left.

"This is all your fault."

Touka kicked Kaneki's foot out of frustration as they walked. Since the idea of going to the library in the first place had been his, Kaneki could not argue with her.

"I'm sorry, Hinami," he said. She shook her head. This also hit Kaneki hard.

She probably won't get to go to the library anymore.

But things went the opposite direction.

"Really? She wants to go back?"

When Touka told him that Hinami wanted to go to the library, it was not long before the due date for the books she'd checked out.

"She says if I'm out of the house, the time goes by just like *that* when she reads the books she got from the library," Touka said, drumming her fingers in frustration on the counter at Anteiku. "Even though the more she's around humans the more chance she has of something bad happening again. You know what, Kaneki? You really are a pro at making trouble."

If it had been up to Touka, going to the library would have been a one-time-only thing, regardless of how Hinami felt.

But I think she feels that she owes it to Hinami. Even Touka can see the contradiction of her heading off to school while Hinami sits at home, hungry for knowledge.

"So what are we gonna do?"

"She wants to go back no matter what, so I guess we're going to take her."

Touka's entire body exuded disgust, but the plan was made: the three of them would go back to the library.

"Hurry up and choose so we can get back home, Hinami," Touka said as soon as they'd arrived at the library, to hurry her along.

This time they went on a Saturday instead, in hopes of avoiding contact with humans as much as possible.

Hinami nodded obediently and ran off. Evidently she was looking for the sequel to a book she had borrowed the other day.

But despite the nasty memory of the last visit, as long as she had a stack of books in front of her she was a bubbling fountain of curiosity.

"Mr. Kaneki, what kind of book is this one?"

"Oh, this is a British fantasy novel. It's so popular they made it into a movie."

"And this one? Is it funny?"

"Hmm, just a second, let me have a look inside."

As this trivial back-and-forth repeated itself over and over again, the time passed.

"Hey, Hinami, have you decided yet?"

"Yeah."

By the time she finally decided which books she wanted to check out, it had been over an hour. Kaneki could feel Touka's irritation as they headed to the counter.

"Hey, you!"

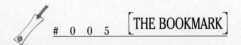

0 0 5 [THE BOOKMARK]

Just then they heard someone call out from the other side of the bookshelves. Kaneki, Touka, and Hinami all turned to look.

"Oh, it's you."

Standing there was the boy who had said those heartless words to Hinami when they first came to the library.

Hinami's body stiffened immediately.

"Kid, you've got a lot of nerve . . ."

The boy was frightened of Touka for a second, but then he turned to Hinami and said, "I'm sorry about before." He bowed his head. "I didn't mean to bully you, I just asked because I didn't understand. I told my dad later and he told me off. He told me that some kids can't go to school because they're sick . . . So I'm sorry. Please accept my apology."

The boy ran over to Hinami and held something out to her. "Here," he said.

Kaneki looked over from where he stood to see what was in the boy's hand. "A bookmark?"

The bookmark was silver and shaped like a spatula, with a four-leaf clover engraved at the end.

The boy looked puzzled by Hinami, who stood there stiffly not taking his gift, but she eventually stuck it in one of the books she was carrying.

"Okay, bye," the boy said, running off. All Hinami could do was watch him walk away in a daze.

As they walked home Hinami took the lead. "This is really bad," Touka said, quietly enough that Hinami couldn't hear.

The boy remembered her. This was a real problem for them, because a child that age would talk about anything that happened to him without a care. And apparently he'd talked to his parents about Hinami. So now there was a possibility of the story getting around where it shouldn't.

Kaneki also had complicated feelings about it. As much as he wished for Ghouls and humans to get along, there was—practically speaking—a big, steep wall standing between them.

"Mr. Kaneki! Hey, Mr. Kaneki, look how pretty it is . . ." Hinami said, holding the bookmark up in the light.

"You're right," Kaneki said. A complicated expression crossed Touka's face.

After that, Hinami seemed to treat the bookmark the boy had given her with the utmost care.

When the due date for her books got close she would start begging to go back to the library, and they frequently ran into the boy who had given it to her. He seemed to come to the library a lot, perhaps because he loved books.

He was younger than Hinami, but he treated her like a big brother would and sometimes taught her words instead of Kaneki.

It made for a delightful scene, but Touka's expression was cloudy, and Kaneki looked on in confusion too. *What is the correct thing to do here?*

The boy sat down beside Hinami, and they began to read a book together. Relieved from his post, Kaneki sat a short distance away and watched the two of them.

He decided to look at a newspaper to pass the time. Page after page was devoted to extensive coverage of another incident involving a Ghoul.

"... was a female nurse working at the university hospital in the 20th Ward, who was apparently just married ..."

She had gone missing just before her honeymoon, but when they found her they made a horrible discovery.

"I wonder what they mean—'suffered extensive damage to the skin.' Was her skin torn off, or ... ?"

"Strange way of eating. I don't care what they say, it's gotta be that guy again," Touka said. She was sitting next to Kaneki, looking at Hinami with obvious boredom.

"Someone you know?"

"I don't know."

It certainly seemed like she *did* know, but he didn't feel like responding to her. Kaneki folded the paper up and returned it to where it had been.

"Hold up."

Just then, Touka grabbed his arm to stop him.

"What is it?"

"Just shut up."

Touka half rose to her feet. She was staring as if she were look-ing for something. *Could we really be in imminent danger?* Kaneki gulped hard and looked in the direction she was looking.

When he did, he saw a woman approaching them. She looked like she was probably a college student too. She had long, black hair, and when she reached point-blank range, she said to Touka, "Oh, you come to the library too, huh."

At first glance she looked like an average woman, but Kaneki knew from Touka's defensive demeanor that she must be a Ghoul, too.

"She's the girlfriend of the guy who got killed near Anteiku the other day."

"What?!" Touka's explanation provoked an outburst from Kaneki without thinking.

"I wasn't," she said, rejecting it, but her expression never changed. "He just told everyone I was. He knew where I go to college, and he tried to blackmail me into giving him 'food' by threatening to expose me there. I'm glad he's dead."

She sat down next to Touka, who also quit being on guard and sat back down.

"Kizayaro is so violent, though."

Is that the name of the guy who did the crime we were reading about in the paper? Kizayaro?

"Yeah, sounds like it. We were in the same class in middle and

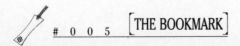

high school but we don't really hang out now so I don't really know him. Anyway, forget about that—this is Kaneki, right? The kid I've heard so much about. This is the first time we've spoken, isn't it?"

"Nice to meet you . . ."

After the battle with the Ghoul investigators, there had been widespread rumors that Kaneki had defeated a dove. It seemed like she'd heard them too.

But when Kaneki bowed his head to her, she remained expressionless.

"Nagachika's a smart kid, isn't he," she said.

How does she know Hide's name?

It was Kaneki's turn to be tense.

"We were active together a while back," she said.

"'Active?' What do you mean by that?"

"It's better not to get into it. Anyway, it wasn't a big deal. And it's got nothing to do with what I want to do to you now," she said without any inflection as she ran her fingers through her long black hair. Her eyes turned to Hinami.

"I thought you didn't seem like the type to go to the library, Touka, but I see you came for the girl's sake. You shouldn't have."

"Why not?"

Touka knit her eyebrows at the girl's frank way of speaking.

The girl stood up. "Clever people shouldn't get too near Ghouls. And Ghouls who can't lie shouldn't get too near humans," she said, looking down at Kaneki and Touka. "Otherwise all you're doing is spreading misery."

What does that mean? Kaneki wondered. He looked to Touka, who was grimacing as if she'd just realized something.

"And you too, Kaneki."

"Me?"

She turned her attack on Kaneki. *But I'm definitely no good at lying either.*

However, she had more on her mind than just Ghouls who can't lie.

"I don't have a lot of friends, so maybe I'm not a good point of comparison, but . . . you should take a more objective look at Nagachika's abilities. His sensitivity winds up giving him insights into things you couldn't see to begin with."

What she said was similar to what Nishiki Nishio had said, before he'd caused harm to Kaneki and Hide.

Hide's words and actions were idiotic, but he could see the world around him clearly. Keeping close to a human with that kind of ability was dangerous for a Ghoul like Kaneki, she said.

"Sankou, what the hell's gotten into you? Why would you say that?" Touka cut in. Sankou tilted her head to one side.

"Just out of the goodness of my

heart. I mean, it's thanks to Kaneki here that things have gone back to normal. It's been fun talking like a friend to people who might be mistaken for being my own age," she said, then quietly added, "I'm very grateful to Nagachika too."

Then, saying, "Well, I've done all I could," she left Kaneki and Touka, who were still confused.

"W-what was she talking about?"

Kaneki couldn't make heads or tails of it. He looked at Touka.

"I dunno. Sankou isn't the fighting kind, and I think she's fine as long as she's left alone. She might look tough, but she rarely talks in front of humans and goes to great lengths not to be seen, and she's the kind who hides her bad side too."

But Touka stood up and walked toward Hinami anyway, as if something in the girl's words was pulling her there.

"'Spreading misery?'"

Left on his own, Kaneki turned the phrase over in his head.

III

"Okay, today we're going home right away!"

It was the millionth time the three of them had gone to the library together. Touka said her catchphrase, and Hinami ran off into the shelves. The boy didn't seem to be there that day. Touka was relieved at that.

And Kaneki, for his part, stood next to Touka, watching Hinami picking out books. Every time he watched her happily selecting a book, he was glad they'd brought her, but he still had Sankou's words in his mind.

Some lies had to be told in order for a Ghoul to blend in with the human world.

First, that you were not a Ghoul. And to tell that lie, the biggest one, there were hundreds of little lies that had to be told.

Hinami was innocent, obedient, and a good kid. She was not used to the game of telling lies, pretending she was something else, and taking people for a ride. To her, such an act was bad in and of itself.

The boy had not tried to find out why Hinami couldn't read very well, but the day would eventually come when Hinami had to lie. Thinking about it gave Kaneki some very complicated feelings.

Lost in his thoughts, Kaneki suddenly heard a hysterical voice behind him.

"Wait, what—what are you . . ."

Touka, who was standing next to him, started to shake in response.

"Yoriko?!" she stuttered.

Kaneki turned around to see Touka's friend Yoriko.

She was panicking like she'd seen something she wasn't supposed to see.

"I-I'm sorry, Touka, I didn't mean to butt in! I was just surprised . . ." Yoriko started defending herself in a fluster.

"No, no!" Touka looked drawn.

"It's okay, see you at school!"

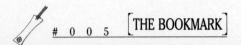

0 0 5 [THE BOOKMARK]

"Yoriko, wait! Yoriko!"

Yoriko rushed off, and Touka chased after her.

"You idiot! This is all your fault! And it's your problem to solve!" Touka yelled at Kaneki, who was standing there, flabbergasted. Without any idea what was going on, he followed the two of them.

"Hello? Touka? Mr. Kaneki?"

Hinami came back, her arms full of books, to find the two of them gone. She looked around but they were nowhere to be seen.

"Where'd you go?"

She put her books down on a chair and ran off looking for them.

Five minutes later, Kaneki and Touka came back, done with playing the chasing game with Yoriko.

"She was too quick. And all that running around . . ."

"I don't think the problem got solved, either."

They had caught up with Yoriko, but whatever Touka tried to say, Yoriko just kept repeating, "It's fine, I didn't see anything." It looked like there was no way to solve the "misunderstanding" after all. Touka frowned.

"Oh, looks like she's found some books."

Kaneki gestured to the stack of children's books near where he was sitting. Touka picked the books up and looked toward the bookshelves.

"I guess she's still looking . . ."

They sat there next to each other, waiting unquestioningly for Hinami.

"Touka? Mr. Kaneki?"

Unaware that the two of them had gone back to where they were before, Hinami left the library and wandered the streets in search of them.

"Where are they?"

Tears of fear welled up in her eyes, and she wiped them away. This was the kind of worry she had always caused her mom and dad. She knew she had to be strong on her own.

"Hey!" someone yelled at Hinami, who had stopped in the middle of the road trying to stop crying. She took her hands away from her eyes and looked up to see some rough-looking high school kids standing there.

"Get your head outta the clouds, brat!" they shouted at her. Hinami was frozen with fear.

"S-sorry," she stuttered.

They laughed and jeered at her.

"Think you got it bad now? You should come with us..."

The teens surrounded Hinami, staring at her as if they were sizing her up. Overcome by fear, she tried to run away, but they grabbed her arm.

"Oh, where do you think you're going?"

"S-stop... please," she said.

"She sounds cute too," one said, cackling.

"No way, man, she's just a kid. You a pedophile or something?"

"Look, my big brother and sister are..."

"Hey, what'd you call me? Shut up, man. You're coming with us."

They didn't listen to a word Hinami said. Instead, they started dragging her off somewhere.

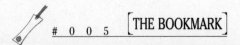 # 0 0 5 [THE BOOKMARK]

What do I do? What do I do?

Hinami was panicking but people kept walking past her quickly.

"Wait . . ."

Among all those people, only one stopped. It was the boy who had given Hinami the bookmark. He had seen Hinami surrounded by the group of teens. And he could see that they were trying to take Hinami somewhere she didn't want to go.

"Where's your big brother and sister?!" he said, looking around, but there was no sign of the two people he'd always seen with her.

"P-please help, I think they're bullying that girl!" He started begging nearby adults for help. But they were all in a hurry and wouldn't pay any attention.

"What do I do?"

They were trying to drag Hinami across the street by the arm. The boy took a step toward them.

But there were five of the boys, and they were much bigger and taller than him.

He took a step back. Then he turned around and started running.

"I'm sorry!" the boy yelled, running away from the scene.

"She's taking a while, don't you think?"

Around that time, Touka had started getting suspicious that Hinami was taking so long. She stood up and started looking for her. Kaneki checked in Hinami's favorite corner, but she was nowhere to be seen.

"Find her?"

"No, she's not there."

Touka's face darkened before Kaneki's eyes. Hinami had been at risk due to her own carelessness before, and she was upset that the same thing might have happened again.

"Let's have another look," Kaneki said, masking his worry. "I'm sure she'll turn up." Touka nodded and went off to search the library again.

"Sir, Miss!"

Just then, they heard a cry too loud for the quiet library. Everyone turned to look out of curiosity, as did Kaneki and Touka. There they saw the boy. He ran up to them, tears streaming down his cheeks and panting. His obvious distress told them it was an emergency.

"What's wrong? What happened?"

"She's—she's on the other street, and some scary people have got her..."

The words "scary people" suggested to them either Ghoul investigators or Ghouls.

"Hinami!" Touka started running immediately.

"I'll take you!"

She grabbed the boy's hand as she passed him. Kaneki also started running at full speed. There were lots of people on the street so Touka couldn't make use of her full capabilities. But the fact that there were lots of people around also meant something else.

If the investigators have got her, they'll evacuate the area before they attack... But everything seems normal. So maybe it's not the investigators.

But Touka had the boy with her. Kaneki couldn't use the word "investigators" so carelessly around him.

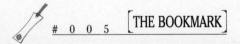 # 0 0 5 [THE BOOKMARK]

"Hey, Touka, I don't think it's those guys, you know!" he shouted.

But Touka shouted back, "What guys?" She was completely lacking in calm.

When they got to the road, the boy pointed a little farther down.

"There she is—there!"

"Hinami!"

As they ran down the road they saw Hinami ahead of them, surrounded by a group of boys from a nearby school. Not investigators, not Ghouls, just a group of humans. Nonetheless, Touka's anger bubbled up at the sight of Hinami sobbing in fear.

Her eyes turned bright red.

She's gonna kill them.

The moment he realized that, he yelled, "All we need to do is save her! That's enough!"

We're not here to kill anyone, we're here to rescue her.

"What're you doing?"

The teens turned around. Touka's red eyes went away just in the nick of time. She dropped the boy's hand and stormed over.

"Wha—"

Touka pushed her way into the group like a galloping beast. The boys' eyes grew wide with surprise as she grabbed Hinami and got back out before they could even reach for her.

"H-hey! What're you doing?!" the boys finally yelled, dumbfounded, as they started to move in on them. Kaneki put himself between the teens and Touka.

"Touka, take Hinami and the boy and get away from here."

"I'm gonna kill them."

"Touka, no!"

She let Hinami down from her arms and started going for the group of boys, but Kaneki's voice stopped her. He spoke to her harshly.

"For Hinami's sake, get her and the boy out of here."

If her true form was revealed, she would kill people to keep her secret. If she killed the teens then and there, that might include the boy. And who knew what that would do to Hinami.

"I'm begging you," he said, pleading with her. Finally regaining her composure, Touka clicked her tongue, grabbed Hinami and the boy by the hand, and ran off.

"Hey, wait!"

"Just stop!"

Kaneki spread his arms out to stop the boys, who were trying to run after them.

"Who the hell are you, man?"

"I'm a friend of theirs. There's no need to be violent, so stop. Let's talk it over."

The boys turned and looked at each other.

"You making fun of us?!" they yelled as they started to hit him. Kaneki took their punches. He rolled to the ground from the momentum and wound up flat on his stomach. His teeth bit into his cheeks hard, where the boys couldn't see. His teeth cut into his flesh and pain ran through the cuts, but he bore it. Then, keeping his mouth shut, he stood up.

"Hey, give it up!"

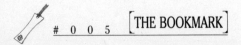

Another boy punched Kaneki in the stomach.

Perfect.

Kaneki grabbed his stomach and bent over as he opened his mouth. When he did, all the spit and blood he'd been holding in his mouth came out at once. It looked like a cheap horror movie effect, but the blood made the teens recoil.

"H-hey . . ."

Kaneki coughed exaggeratedly, spitting out blood, as he fell to the ground.

"Whoaaaaa!"

The boys started yelling in panic. One of them, seeing Kaneki thrashing on the ground, said, "Guys, this is bad." As if that was their signal, they started yelling, "Never seen him before!" "Leave me alone!" Then they ran away.

"Well, that went better than I thought."

Kaneki stood up, swallowing the blood he hadn't already spit out. All the blood looked impressive, but thanks to the training he'd received from Touka and Yomo, he wasn't in too much pain.

"So doing it your way worked out . . ."

When things had calmed down, Touka came back, amazed.

"Mr. Kaneki, I'm sorry . . ." Hinami's eyes were full of tears, however.

"I'm fine," Kaneki said, smiling.

"The kid told us what happened," Touka said, looking at the boy. He was trembling unnaturally. "We wouldn't have found her if it wasn't for you."

"But I didn't do anything!" the boy said, hesitating. "I . . . I . . ."

Kaneki tilted his head. Hinami looked at the boy, tears still in her eyes. He looked back at them, before yelling, as if he'd made up his mind, "My dad told me to stand up to bad people, and I wanted to help, but I was so scared I couldn't do anything! I . . . I . . . just ran away!"

"No, you didn't," Kaneki interrupted. "You helped Hinami in the best way possible. Didn't he?" he said, turning to look at Touka. Her face said *Don't bring me into this*, but then she smiled.

"We found her thanks to you," she said. Kaneki smiled.

"So, thank you."

Kaneki's words cut through the boy's worries, and tears started to overflow from his eyes. He tried to hold the tears back, perhaps out of embarrassment over crying, but he couldn't stop them. Kaneki smiled again at the sight of him trying not to sob.

Hinami started to cry again, brought on by the boy's tears.

All's well that ends well, Kaneki thought to himself, glad from the bottom of his heart.

Just then, Hinami clutched her hands to her stomach and fell to the ground.

"Hinami?"

Touka looked at her hurriedly, but Hinami looked like she had no idea what was happening to her.

"Are you okay?" the boy asked gently, looking down at her and wiping his tears away with his sleeve. Hinami got up, still clutching her stomach. She shook her head slightly and ran away.

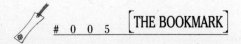 # 0 0 5 [THE BOOKMARK]

"Hinami!"

"Hinami, wait!"

What just happened? Touka chased after her immediately. Kaneki was left speechless for a moment before saying thank you to the boy and running after the two of them.

Hinami ran for a while before stopping suddenly. Both her hands still clutched her stomach.

"Hinami?"

For some reason Touka stopped Kaneki when he tried to call out to the girl out of concern. Then, she stood next to her and called her Hina, her nickname. Hinami did not turn around.

"My stomach . . . started," she said, her voice trembling.

They went cold at once, as if someone had poured a bucket of ice water over them. Basically, what had happened was, to put it simply . . . what?

"I don't know why, but my stomach is . . . why? Why am I . . . ?"

Hinami was in a state of confusion, not understanding what was happening in her own body.

"It's okay, Hinami. It's okay now," Touka said, gathering the girl in her arms. Hinami said nothing else. Neither did the two of them.

There was a large borderline between humans and Ghouls. And the more one knew the starker it stood between them and humans, like a complete mockery.

After that, Hinami didn't want to go to the library anymore. She hid away the bookmark the boy had given her.

This world is wrong.

That's what the young Ghoul investigator Kankei had faced off against had said.

Kaneki thought about those words. *Does he envision a world that has nothing wrong with it?*

But I still . . .

I can't imagine that kind of world.

IV

Kaneki was lost in thought, Touka was worried about Hinami, and Hinami was downbeat. They could all see right through each other.

"It's just like they say, when you're exhausted little problems add up," Yoshimura said with a sigh. He had just gotten word from Yomo.

They never would have left Hinami alone back when he'd warned them about suspicious people hanging around the area. The

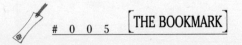

0 0 5 ⌈THE BOOKMARK⌉

suspicious characters hadn't been spotted for a while, so they'd let their guard down.

But strange people in the neighborhood or not, this was unacceptable. If they got complacent and let their attention drift even once, it would all have been for nothing.

The suspicious characters Yoshimura had warned them of had never existed. They had appeared when Yoshimura wanted them to, and Yomo had fleshed them out a little—these shadows, so to speak, that walked on their own.

It was because he worried about them that these shadows appeared, sometimes to protect them and sometimes to hold them back.

"Is it kind, or is it cruel? Sometimes I don't know anymore," Yomo whispered. "Just talking to myself," he added.

Yoshimura gave a graceful smile and said, "If everything was easily understood, this wouldn't really be living." Then, like Yomo, he added, "Just talking to myself."

"There's still things I want to see, you know."

V

"I'm back."

"Hey, honey. You're home early."

Mother walked over to father, just home from work. Father handed her his suit jacket and headed down the hall.

"They've still got me jumping all over the place for a while."

"But you were just going to get a post in the 20th Ward! Well, what a shame."

"That's not all. Toujou's really happy about it. He says if I were posted in the 20th Ward I'd go straight home and never go out drinking with him."

"Oh my," she chuckled.

When he walked into the living room, their son was there reading a book.

"Hey, Yuuki, what are you reading today?" he asked his son, who loved reading. He held up the cover.

"*The New Book of Ghoul Dissection*?"

"Oh, that's nice, honey. Taking an interest in your dad's work?"

"Come on, give me a break. It's a dangerous job fighting these inhuman beasts who prey on people. Just the other day there was a Ghoul spotted in the 20th Ward and we had to—" He began to explain, with a somber look.

"Yes, dear," the mother said, stretching.

"Just joking. Hey, is it dinnertime?"

The two of them went into the kitchen.

Yuuki sighed with relief and stuck a bookmark in his book. It was a silver bookmark with a four-leaf clover engraved at one end.

But those red eyes came back to his mind—the red eyes of the girl's "big sister" when they'd found her. They were like the kakugan that dad was always telling him about, the mark of a Ghoul.

Now that he thought about it, there was a lot about those three that matched up with what his dad had told him about Ghouls.

"Inhuman beasts." That was what his dad always called them.

"Are they really all bad guys, all of them?" he wondered.

The girl had a kindly sister, a brother who kept really cool in a crisis, and the girl herself was so timid but cute when she smiled.

"Or are some of them . . . actually good?"

Yuuki slammed his book shut.

Forget about it.

There's nothing I can do about it now anyway. No matter how bad it looks, until I find the best way, it's . . .

"Yuuki, I was just wondering, whatever happened to the girl you met at the library?" his dad asked, coming back into the living room.

"Huh?" Yuuki said. "Oh, um . . . I think she moved away."

東 京　[DAYS]　喰 種

[YOSHIDA]

Even Kazuo is alive.

This is the story of Kazuo Yoshida's lifetime of struggle, until the final curtain fell on his life at the age of forty-one, struck down by Nishiki as collateral damage when Kaneki, freshly minted as a Ghoul and lured there by the scent of death, stumbled into his feeding spot, panicked, and screamed.

"Okay, everyone, I want those thighs up! And down. And up again, high as you can! Right, here we go—one, two—one, two!"

In the 20th Ward, not far from the main shopping street, was the fitness club where Kazuo worked. It was a busy place full of people coming and going. Kazuo was a member of the staff there, primarily making his living by teaching aerobics.

If one had to say one thing about his face, it would be, "too bad."

But if nothing else, his build was fantastic from working there. His limbs were long, his torso was ripped, and even his butt was tight. His coworkers frequently praised him, saying, "If it wasn't for that face!"

"Kazuo, you really do have a fantastic body, you know. I wish mine was like that," said Manami, a woman who had recently joined the gym. She spoke to him during the break in aerobics with a dreamy look on her face. She apparently worked as a receptionist at a big company, and she was charming and cute. Plus, every time she came to the gym, she complimented Kazuo.

"I think that girl's into you, Kazuo . . ." said Saotome, one of his friends at work, once all the customers had gone home and just the staff was left.

"I—I really don't think so," Kazuo said, and laughed nervously.

"But she doesn't even look at me or anyone else. Looks like the flowers are finally in bloom for you too, Kazuo."

Saotome was mainly in charge of the gym, and he was a popular, attractive guy with a muscular body and something a little bit wild about him. He was much younger than Kazuo, but he had been at the fitness club for longer, so Saotome spoke to him without mincing words. Kazuo was used to it.

"It's just that I'm easy to talk to. She probably only talks to an old guy like me out of pity," Kazuo said in an unassuming way.

"You're probably right!" Saotome agreed straightaway. *I wish he'd tried to deny it.*

But the idea that anything could happen with me and such a young, cute girl . . . Kazuo didn't feel bad about it.

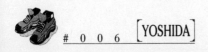

One day, he left the fitness club after work and was heading home when, out of nowhere, he heard someone yelling. The yells seemed to be coming from the parking lot at the club. *Maybe there's a fight happening.*

It would be horrible if there were a problem on the club grounds. Kazuo ran toward the voices.

When he got there, he saw Manami, the girl who always spoke to him. And right by her was a dodgy-looking guy with crimped hair and a goatee. The man had been yelling at Manami.

Kazuo's face might've been a shame, but he was a Ghoul. He was seldom outdone by a human.

"Knock it off!"

Kazuo jumped out.

"Oh? Who the hell are you?"

But the man threatened him and Kazuo backed away.

"P-please stop. It's dark now and you'll disturb the neighbors . . ."

Kazuo had lost his initial momentum and become flustered. The man clicked his tongue.

"Get me that half a million now!" he yelled, then left.

Half a million yen?

"I'm sorry, Kazuo . . ."

"Don't be. What was that . . . ?" Kazuo didn't know if he should ask her about what he'd heard.

"The truth is, my mother is sick, and in order to come up with the money for all the hospital bills, I had to go to a loan shark," said Manami, without him even asking. "But I've got everything under control now! I'm sorry for causing you trouble." She paused. "I'm so glad you came to help me."

"Oh?" he said, sounding nervous and hollow. Manami turned away and left before he realized it. Kazuo thought about the faint blush of her cheeks just then, and squatted back down to the ground for a while.

Some people do terrible things. Imagine the kind of guy who'd try to wring money out of an innocent woman like that.

Once he got home, Kazuo lamented to himself about the absurdities of the world as he did sit-ups.

A guy like that will come back to threaten her again. It might be at home or at work, or even somewhere she likes to hang out, like today. It doesn't matter. To dare causing a scene like that by making somebody scream in public, you've gotta have something wrong with you mentally. Is Manami always in that kind of trouble? Kazuo couldn't let himself think like that. He directed all his anger toward loan sharks.

"Anyone who does that really oughta be killed! I'm gonna kill 'em!"

I mean, I'm a Ghoul, if it comes down to it I could just eat them. Kazuo's eyes turned red, and he started doing his sit-ups even faster. That day, he was so angry he kept doing sit-ups for hours.

II

"Excuse me, Kazuo? I just wanted to say thank you, for before."

A few days later, when the aerobics class had ended and every-one was leaving, Manami got changed quickly and came over to Kazuo to talk.

I did a thousand sit-ups with you on my mind, he thought, but knew it wasn't something he could say to her, so he refrained and said, "Don't worry about it. I hope you're all right."

"I brought a little something for you, to say thanks," she said, and pulled a large lunch box out of her bag. The stench of human food drifted out.

"Is it a . . ."

"It's a lunch box. You work out all day, so I thought you must be hungry. I made lots!"

Sometimes concern takes the form of a one-two punch.

But Kazuo said, "Thank you." This was evidence of her gratitude. *Can I just pretend to eat it? No, no I can't.*

"Take care, have a good day, Kazuo!"

When he got home, Kazuo steeled himself and ate the food. *Awful, awful, awful, all of it awful. But I ate it. I ate the whole thing.*

Then he slept for two days.

A week after that, Kazuo was still in poor physical condition from the shock to the stomach Manami's food had given him. Work was finally over and he was leaving the fitness club when he heard someone shouting in the parking lot.

"Not again!"

He rushed over to find Manami being threatened again by the same man from the other day.

"I said, leave her alone!"

"Not you again . . ."

The man clucked. "Half a million, I told you, half a million!" he spat at Manami, then left.

Then, Kazuo ran over to her.

"Manami, are you okay?"

"Oh, Kazuo!"

Manami collapsed in his arms, clinging to him. Kazuo stood up straight in surprise.

"Oh no, I'm sorry," she said, pulling away as she apologized. "What is there to like about a woman like me . . . A useless woman like me, hounded by collectors with my mother in the hospital—I'm no good for someone like you!"

She ran away in a flood of tears. Kazuo could only stand there, flabbergasted, and watch her leave.

"I'm really gonna kill 'em, gonna kill 'em for real, this is not a metaphor, this is for real!"

For days, Kazuo was shaking with anger when he thought of Manami. In order to calm himself, he went to Anteiku for coffee.

But one day even having a coffee at Anteiku didn't do it for him. His anger toward the loan shark was still burning within him,

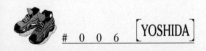

his hair was falling out, and his forehead felt like it had gone dry.

The relatively mild-mannered Kazuo was spitting out his violent mantra, like a drunken human.

Suddenly, Touka Kirishima, the evening shift waitress, emerged from behind the counter and came over to him. She stood beside Kazuo and gave him a grin.

"There are humans and other customers here, I will kill you for real."

Her voice was chilling, a voice that was unimaginable from looking at her smile.

Her kind of 'kill' goes way beyond mine, the most real of the 'for real,' a demon's 'for real.'

Kazuo went silent and started drinking his coffee, because he valued his life.

However, once he had finally calmed down, Kazuo made a decision. *It's time to show that guy.*

III

"Oh, what's this for?"

It was a thick brown envelope. Manami's eyes widened when Kazuo suddenly gave it to her.

"Open it up," he said to her.

She looked inside the envelope cautiously.

Kazuo watched her clasp her hand over her mouth in surprise. He nodded, slowly and quietly.

Inside the envelope was 500,000 yen.

It was the amount she had borrowed from the loan shark.

"You can pay back your loan with it."

"Oh no, Kazuo, I couldn't! I just couldn't let you do something like this!"

"It's okay, really."

Kazuo put both of his thumbs up, forming little brackets.

"I want you to be free from all this."

Manami's eyes were full of tears, which fell silently onto her cheeks. Then she ran off.

Yes, Kazuo thought. *Run, run as fast as you can, run to your freedom!*

After that, Manami disappeared.

Although she was meant to come to two lessons per week, no one had seen her at all.

Maybe she got into a dispute with the loan shark and got in some trouble—

Kazuo regretted not going with her to take care of it.

He snuck a look at her fitness club membership application form and tried to call her on her cell phone. But she did not answer.

Next he went to her address, which was also on the form. But there was no apartment building there.

Where on earth has she gone? Kazuo was visibly exhausted from worrying over her pointlessly.

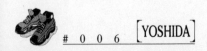

"Hey, man, what's with you? You haven't been with it lately."

His coworker, Saotome, was worried about him. He and the other staff had found Kazuo standing alone in the aerobics room, staring into the mirror. "You can always come to me about things, you know," he said, and smiled, showing his perfect white teeth.

"That's right, Kazuo. If you keep this up your body fat will be down to zero percent."

"We're friends, right? You know you can talk to me about anything."

His other coworkers also gave him worried looks and gentle encouragement.

They're right. It's too much for me to handle on my own now.

"The thing is . . ." Kazuo said, having boldly decided to tell everyone what had happened. His coworkers listened to his story with serious expressions on their faces.

But one after another those expressions hardened.

". . . so I think what happened is, Manami has had something terrible happen to her."

"Kazuo . . ."

As he was finishing his story, Saotome said his name and grabbed him by the shoulders, cutting him off.

"I want you to listen carefully to what I have to say," he said as a preface. "A woman who has borrowed 500,000 yen and whose mother is in the hospital doesn't come to a fitness club."

It was a shock. "What are you saying?" he laughed. But Saotome's words had hit him hard and wouldn't go away. These words floated in his mind: *He's absolutely right!*

"Kazuo, she put on a cute act, but she's going out with a rough-looking guy . . . With the permed hair and the goatee, he's definitely a yakuza."

He hadn't realized she had a boyfriend. Much less one that sounded just like the loan shark who had yelled at her that time—could they be twins?

"And to begin with, if you work for a big company you could pay back 500,000 yen easily."

"I have no idea what's a lie and what's true anymore . . ."

His coworkers started to tell him, one after another, things they had wondered about while they listened to his story. They mentioned minute details Kazuo hadn't noticed. Finally he got the full picture.

Money had been her reason for joining the fitness club in the first place. Her plan had been to find an easy mark, and she'd singled out gullible Kazuo.

"Kazuo! You have to report this to the police! You still have rights, no matter how inexperienced you are with women!" Saotome yelled passionately, his hands balled up into fists. But Kazuo shook his head.

I mean, I want to report it too. I want to take Manami and all of them down. But if I go to the police and something gives me away as a Ghoul while they're taking down the details, I'm screwed—they'll kill me.

Lately, all he could do was cry himself to sleep.

The world blamed everything on Ghouls, but humans aren't

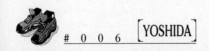

perfect either. And what have I done? Sure, I kill and eat people, but I wish they could see past that.

Kazuo had sunk from sitting to lying down. He had made himself small and rounded from the shock, like a pill bug. He could not move.

"Kazuo," Saotome said, tapping him on the shoulder. "Let's dance."

With his forehead against the floor and his hands on each side of his knees, Kazuo looked just like he was in the yoga position called child pose. He turned his head to look at Saotome.

"Don't tell me you've forgotten this fitness club's motto . . . 'Hard times and sad times may come but . . .'"

Saotome reached out to Kazuo to give him a hand up. All his coworkers stood as well and joined voices to say, "'. . . but if you get out of breath and sweaty . . .'"

Kazuo looked up at them. Everyone was smiling at him.

He clenched his lips together, took Saotome's hand, and stood up.

"'. . . all your problems will float away!'" Kazuo shouted. Saotome's white smile gleamed as he pointed upward.

"Okay, put some music on for Kazuo, guys! Kaz, you're gonna be in the middle, of course! Show me some aerobics with soul!"

Kazuo nodded intently and took his place in the middle. Someone put some fast-paced music on.

"All right everybody, I want those hands up! Be careful not to hit your neighbors!"

"Okay!"

"Now take a deep breath, then release. And then one more time!"

"Okay!"

"Right, everybody ready? One, two, one, two, one, two, three, four!"

Kazuo danced.

He danced with all his might. Sweat was flying off of him, and he was drenched in it. But his coworkers didn't point this out to him. They just kept yelling, "One, two! One, two!"

Kazuo was wounded. But somehow, it didn't matter to him

so much anymore. Tomorrow he might feel down again, but for now he was happy.

The next day, he was sobbing his eyes out over a coffee at Anteiku. Sure enough, Kazuo wanted to die every time he thought about the 500,000 yen he'd lost, and to keep his sanity he had latched on to his mantra: *I'll kill 'em, seriously one day I'll kill 'em.*

"I heard there've been suspicious sightings in the area."

"Again?"

That's when he overheard the staff talking about something dangerous. He looked over and saw the meek expressions on their faces. *Did something happen?*

Just then, the manager, Yoshimura, passed by.

"Has something happened? I keep hearing all this talk about suspicious people around . . ."

Yoshimura stopped. "Don't worry," he said, with his usual gentle smile. "They will not be seen near you."

They won't be seen near me? What does that mean?

But Yoshimura just grinned and did not say anything else.

Somehow, he felt like he'd been told not to intervene any further. Kazuo laughed drily for a long time, then turned his gaze to the window.

Even I got tangled up with Manami and a suspicious character, but I doubt anyone would pay attention if I told them.

Even I keep on living with all my heart.

Such were his thoughts on a balmy late afternoon.

TOKYO
GHOUL

It's been an honor to have been involved with making the novelization of Tokyo Ghoul happen after having been a fan since its origins as a serial. Thank you so much.

–**Shin Towada**

Thank you!
sui